THIS PUFFIN MODERN CLASSIC
BELONGS TO

____

To my Brother

Some reviews of *Smith*

'. . . a graphic, breathtaking picture of England – and particularly of London – with a handful of memorable, larger-than-life characters'
– *Who's Who of Children's Literature*

'An excellent way to introduce children to Leon Garfield's wonderful historical writing'
– *Independent*

'. . . a train of deceits, double-deceits and theatrically lost documents, the language has a bold glitter . . .'
– *The Times*

'. . . an outstanding work of children's fiction, tough-minded and pungently vivid, with Smith himself a successor to Oliver Twist and Huckleberry Finn' – *Observer*

Books by Leon Garfield

SHAKESPEARE'S STORIES
SHAKESPEARE'S STORIES II
SMITH

PUFFIN MODERN CLASSICS

Smith

Leon Garfield was born in Brighton and educated at Brighton Grammar School. His brief art studies were interrupted by the outbreak of the Second World War. After serving in the medical corps for five years, he returned to England with his author and artist wife, Vivien Alcock, whom he met in Belgium. He worked part-time as a hospital technician until literary success enabled him to devote himself entirely to writing. His books have won many awards including the Guardian Award for Children's Literature and the Carnegie Medal, and some have been dramatized for film and television. For many years he lived with his wife in Highgate, the setting for many of his novels.

Leon Garfield died in 1996, aged 74.

LEON GARFIELD

Smith

Illustrated by Kenny McKendry

PUFFIN

PUFFIN BOOKS

Published by the Penguin Group
Penguin Books Ltd, 80 Strand, London WC2R 0RL, England
Penguin Group (USA), Inc., 375 Hudson Street, New York, New York 10014, USA
Penguin Books Australia Ltd, 250 Camberwell Road, Camberwell, Victoria 3124, Australia
Penguin Books Canada Ltd, 10 Alcorn Avenue, Toronto, Ontario, Canada M4V 3B2
Penguin Books India (P) Ltd, 11 Community Centre, Panchsheel Park, New Delhi – 110 017, India
Penguin Group (NZ), cnr Airborne and Rosedale Roads, Albany, Auckland 1310, New Zealand
Penguin Books (South Africa) (Pty) Ltd, 24 Sturdee Avenue, Rosebank 2196, South Africa

Penguin Books Ltd, Registered Offices: 80 Strand, London WC2R 0RL, England

www.penguin.com

First published by Constable 1967
Published in Puffin Books 1968
Published in this edition 1994, 2004
5

Set in 11/16.25 pt Linotype Palatino
Typeset by Rowland Phototypesetting Ltd, Bury St Edmunds, Suffolk
Made and printed in England by Clays Ltd, St Ives plc

British Library Cataloguing in Publication Data
A CIP catalogue record for this book is available from the British Library

ISBN 0-141-31971-2

Introduction

by Julia Eccleshare

Puffin Modern Classics series editor

Following Smith, or Smut as he is affectionately known to his sisters, through the twists and turns of the dark alleys of London is a roller coaster of an adventure. From the moment that Smith steals a document that others are willing to kill for, it's full of shivery moments.

Whatever is happening, there are so many unknowns. Is the pick-pocketing Smith good or bad? Does he befriend the blind Magistrate Mr Mansfield out of kindness or cunning? Is the highwayman Lord Toby truly his best friend or a double-crossing knave? The fun of *Smith* and much of Leon Garfield's skill lie in his ability to make you change what you think about everything from one moment to the next. Only one thing remains constant. You never, ever, stop liking Smith and admiring him for his determination.

Dirty, thieving Smith is a heart-warming character who lives on his wits, which are fortunately very sharp indeed. Cuffed and cursed all his life, he never loses the cunning instinct that keeps him ahead of his enemies. Nor does he lose his determination, which keeps him turning over every stone until he finds exactly what he wants.

But while it's Smith whose adventures are so intriguing, London – the place where it all happens – makes an equally fascinating backdrop. Leon Garfield leads you through the dirty and crowded back streets where the smells linger in the air; he takes you right into the heart of Newgate Prison, full of an amiable crowd of criminals who enjoy a kind of high life of drinking, smoking and joking even as they wait for their deaths. But he makes you feel just at home in the world of the rich. The contrast in styles is huge, but carriages and servants only disguise a world that is just as corrupt as that out on the streets. Taken together, and described in Leon Garfield's richly evocative language, the two sides of long-ago London are immediate and alive. Those who are as brave as Smith can dare to explore it with him.

Chapter 1

He was called Smith and was twelve years old. Which, in itself, was a marvel; for it seemed as if the smallpox, the consumption, brain-fever, gaol-fever and even the hangman's rope had given him a wide berth for fear of catching something. Or else they weren't quick enough.

Smith had a turn of speed that was remarkable, and a neatness in nipping down an alley or vanishing in a court that had to be seen to be believed. Not that it was often seen, for Smith was rather a sooty spirit of the violent and ramshackle Town, and inhabited the tumbledown mazes about fat St Paul's like the subtle air itself. A rat was like a snail beside Smith, and the most his thousand victims ever got of him was the powerful whiff of his passing and a cold draught in their dexterously emptied pockets.

Only the sanctimonious birds that perched on the church's dome ever saw Smith's progress entire, and as their beady eyes followed him, they chattered savagely, '*Pick*-pocket! *Pick*-pocket! Jug him! Jug-jug-jug him!' as if they'd been appointed by the Town to save it from such as Smith.

His favourite spot was Ludgate Hill, where the world's coaches, chairs and curricles were met and locked, from morning to night, in a horrible, blasphemous confusion. And here, in one or other of the ancient doorways, he leaned and grinned while the shouting and cursing and scraping and raging went endlessly, hopelessly on – till, sooner or later, something prosperous would come his way.

At about half past ten of a cold December morning an old gentleman got furiously out of his carriage, in which he'd been trapped for an hour, shook his red fist at his helpless coachman and the roaring but motionless world, and began to stump up Ludgate Hill.

'*Pick*-pocket! *Pick*-pocket!' shrieked the cathedral birds in a fury.

A country gentleman – judging by his complexion, his clean old-fashioned coat and his broad-legged, lumbering walk which bumped out his pockets in a manner most provoking.

Smith twitched his nose and nipped neatly along like a shadow . . .

The old man's pace was variable: sometimes it was brisk for his years, then he'd slow down, hesitate, look about him – as if the Town had changed much since last he'd visited and he was now no longer confident of his way. He took one turning, then another; stopped, scratched the crisp edge of his wig, then eyed the sallow, seedy city gentry as if to ask the way, till he spied another turn, nodded, briskly took it – and came straight back into Ludgate Hill . . .

A dingy fellow creaked out of a doorway, like he was hinged on it, and made to accost the old man: but he did not. He'd glimpsed Smith. Looks had been exchanged, shoulders shrugged – and the old villain gave way to the young one.

On went the old gentleman, confident now in

his bearings, deeper and deeper into the musty, tottering forest of the Town where Smith hunted fastest and best.

Now a sharpish wind sprang up, and the cathedral birds eyed the leaden sky (which looked too thick and heavy to admit them), screeched, and flew to the lower eminence of Old Bailey. Here, they set up a terrific commotion with their legal brethren, till both Church and Law became absorbed in watching the progress of Smith.

'*Pick*-pocket! *Pick*-pocket! Jug-jug-jug him!'

The old gentleman was very deep in Smith's country now, and paused many a time to peer down the shambling lanes and alleys. Then he'd shake his head vaguely and touch at his coat pocket – as if a queer, deep sense had warned him of a pair of sharp eyes fairly cutting into the cloth like scissors. At last he saw something familiar – some landmark he'd remembered – Godliman Street. Yes: he was in Godliman Street . . .

As suddenly as it had sprung up, the wind died – and the cathedral birds flew back to their dome.

'*Pick*-pocket! *Pick*-pocket!'

The old gentleman began to stump very particularly down Godliman Street, eyeing the old, crumbly houses that were lived in by God knew how many quiet, mysterious souls. And, as he went, he seemed to have two shadows – his own and another, a thin cautious shadow that was not so much seen as sensed . . .

This was the deepest heart of Smith's forest, hidden even from the cathedral birds. Here, the houses reared and clustered as if to shut out the sky, and so promoted the growth of the flat, pale and unhealthy moon-faces of the clerks and scriveners, glimpsed in their dark caves through dusty windows, silent and intent.

Now came a slit between two such properties, a quiet way roofed over at first-floor level: Curtis Alley, leading to Curtis Court.

Framed by the darkness of its alley, Curtis Court presented a grey and peaceful brightness – a neglected clearing in the forest of the Town, where nothing grew, and all save one of the enclosed houses had had their eyes put out with bricks (on account of the tax).

As the old gentleman's steps echoed in the alley, a solitary, dusty raven flew up out of the court with a bitter croak.

Suddenly, the old gentleman gave an involuntary shudder, as if someone – something – had swiftly passed him by and made a draught.

'Someone's walked over me grave!' he muttered, shook his head and entered Curtis Court.

'Beg pardon, sir! Beg pardon –'

Out of a doorway on the left of the court came Smith. Which was the first time the old man had ever laid eyes on him; though all the way from Ludgate Hill there'd never been more than two yards between them.

He stopped, flustered, about six paces from the end of the alley. Which way was the damned urchin going? This way? That way? Angrily he shifted, and Smith, with a quaint clumsiness, brushed against him, and – it was done! In an instant! Smith had emptied the old gentleman's pocket of –

He halted. His eyes glittered sharply. Footsteps in the alley! It would be blocked! He changed direction as briefly as a speck in the wind – and vanished back into his doorway. But so quickly that, seconds after he'd disappeared, the old gentleman was still staggering and bewildered.

Out of the alley came two men in brown. Curious fellows of a very particular aspect – which Smith knew well. Uneasily, he scowled – and wished he might vanish through the crumbling bricks.

The old gentleman had recovered himself. He

stared round angrily – till courtesy got the better of him.

'Good day to ye, gentlemen!' he said, with an apologetic smile.

The newcomers glanced quickly across the court towards the house that had kept one window, and grinned.

'And good day to *you*!'

They moved very neat, and with no commotion. They were proficient in their trade. The taller came at the old man from the front; the other took on his back – and slid a knife into it.

The old gentleman's face was fatefully towards a certain dark doorway. He seemed to peer very anxiously round the heavy shoulder of the man who was holding him – as if for a better view. His eyes flickered with pain at the knife's quick prick. Then he looked surprised – amazed, even – as he felt the cold blade slip into his warm heart.

'Oh! Oh! Oh my –' he murmured, gave a long sigh – and died.

His last sight on this earth had been of a small, wild and despairing face whose flooded eyes shone out of the shadows with all the dread and pity they were capable of.

(Smith was only twelve and, hangings apart, had seen no more than three men murdered in all his life.)

They say that murdered men's eyes keep the image of their last sight for – for how long? Do they take it, hereafter, up to the Seat of Judgement? Smith shivered. He'd no wish for his face to be shown in any place of judgement – in this world or the next!

In a terror as violent as his dislike, he watched the two men in brown. They were dragging the luckless old gentleman towards the darkness of the alley. (Why hadn't he stayed in the country where he'd belonged? What business had he to come stumping – so stupid and defenceless – into Smith's secret forest?)

Now Smith could hear the quick, fumbling sounds of searching; methodical gentry. Still no commotion. Oh, they knew what they were at! But the sounds grew harsh and hasty. Even irritable. Muttered one, 'God rot the old fool! He ain't got it!'

Came a new sound. A very queer one. A tapping, limping scraping sound – as of a lame man's foot-steps on the cobbles. Then a soft, gentlemanly voice.

'Well?'

'Nothing – nothing, yer honour!'

'Liars! Fools! Look again!'

Again the sounds of searching – accompanied by strained, indrawn breath.

'Told you so. Nothing.'

A groan: a very dreadful affair.

'Again! Again! It *must* be there!'

'Well, it ain't, yer honour! And if we stays much longer, we'll be on our way to join 'im . . . on the end of a rope! Come – let's be off.'

'Again! Search once more!'

'With respect – do it yerself, sir.'

'No!'

'Then we're off! Quick! Quick! There's someone coming –'

There was a scuffling and scraping, then the alley and court were momentarily quiet. A shadow crossed the broken, moss-piped paving. It was the raven, making ready to return.

But Smith did not move yet. Voices and clustering footsteps could be heard coming from the far side of the alley. The pale-faced clerks and scriveners and thin-necked attorneys had caught the scent of spilt blood. They'd come out of their rooms and chambers to congregate solemnly and stare.

(But no one came out from the houses within

the court; not even from the house with the single window.)

Now the crowd had grown and oozed into the court itself. The raven flapped sourly up to a gable and croaked with a sardonic air; Smith had invisibly joined the outskirts of the crowd, muttering away with the best of them; then he was through, like a needle through shoddy, to Godliman Street and beyond.

As he went, a door opened in the court, and someone came quietly out . . .

A quarter mile off, on the other side of St Paul's, Smith stopped running. He sat on some steps and fumbled in his ragged, ancient coat. What had he got this time? Something valuable. Something that had been worth the old gentleman's life.

He fished it out. A document. *A document?* Smith stood up, swore, spat and cursed. For, though he was quicker than a rat, sharper than a stoat, foxier than a fox, though he knew the Town's corners and alleys and courts and by-ways better than he knew his own heart, and though he could vanish into the thick air in the twinkling of an eye, he lacked one necessary quality for the circumstance in hand. He could not read. Not so much as a word!

Chapter 2

Darkness came prematurely to the Town, owing to the sun's habit of vanishing into the tall chimney pots of Hanover Square – where, for all Smith knew, it blazed away in the rich parlours till the time came for it to be trundled off to Wapping and begin its course anew.

By four o'clock, the dome of St Paul's stood black and surly against the darkening sky, and its huge shadow was flung eastward over the narrow streets and lanes of that part of the Town.

At last Smith gave up his efforts to force the cramped and awkward ink-lines to yield up their secret. For the light was gone and his eyes, wits and soul were aching with strain. A hundred stratagems had presented themselves to him – and a hundred stratagems he'd rejected. He'd thought of applying to the various scholars of his acquaintance . . . but which one could he trust? He'd thought of cutting the document into its various lines – or even words – and giving each of them to a different reader. But what if he muddled the order, or lost something that proved to be vital?

He walked; he sat; he tramped as far as the churchyard in Old Street, where he leaned up against a headstone, puffed at his short clay pipe, and fished out the document yet again. He stared; he screwed up his eyes and face till he looked like an old walnut, but the dim air and his own dark ignorance made the document seem like the last will and testament of a very old, very lame, very inky spider – on its weary way home.

So Smith likewise, with a deep sigh, packed up his thoughts and went home.

Between Saffron Hill and Turnmill Street stood – or, rather slouched – the Red Lion Tavern. A very evil-looking, tumbledown structure, weatherboarded on three sides and bounded on the fourth by the great Fleet Ditch, which stank and gurgled and gurgled and stank by day and night, like the parlour of the Tavern itself.

This parlour was an ill-lit, noxious place, full of hoarse secrets and red-eyed morsels – not so much from all walks as from all falls of life. Thieves, pick-pockets, foot-pads, unlucky swindlers and ruined gamblers boozed and snoozed here, and were presided over by a greasy landlord who never sold a customer to the gallows for less than a guinea.

Here was Smith's home. Not in the dignity of the parlour itself, but in the cellar below it where he lodged with his sisters, Miss Bridget and Miss Fanny.

'Not nubbed yet?' remarked the landlord humorously, as Smith humped broodily in.

Smith, his head full of darker things than even the Red Lion Tavern, made no answer.

'I spoke to you, Smith.'

'Did you now! I thought it was a belch from the old Ditch!'

Two or three customers grinned, and Smith dodged deftly past the landlord to the cellar steps, but was not quite quick enough to miss a fist on his ear. He howled and vanished . . . and the landlord laughed fit to burst.

'Got him that time!'

'You asked for it! You brought it on yourself!' remarked Miss Bridget, looking up from stitching a brown velveteen coat.

'Poor little Smut!' murmured Miss Fanny, over a pair of grey breeches. 'One day he'll come down them steps stone dead!'

'*I'm* not complaining,' said Smith, rubbing his ear which, had it been clean, would have been red as a strawberry, but instead was now a warm black. 'Saw an old gent done in today.'

'Indeed? And what's that to do with abusing the landlord?'

'Me mind was on other things.'

''Tis no excuse! We brung you up to be genteel. Fanny and me feels the disgrace.'

'Put a dab of vinegar on your little lug, Smut,' said Miss Fanny. ''Twill take out the sting.'

She mentioned vinegar as there was a quantity of it in the cellar; for the sisters engaged in scouring and cleaning besides making genteel alterations to cast-off clothing from unfortunates who were hanged and so never had a chance to wear their last garments out. The velveteen coat and the grey breeches were bespoken by the hangman himself, for they'd come off a very high-stepping rogue indeed and one everybody was sorry to see nubbed.

'But the law must take its course,' had said Miss Bridget, and, ''Tis an ill wind,' had said Miss Fanny, when Smith brought the garments in.

'Look what I got this time!' said Smith, after he'd wiped his ear with vinegar. He fished out the document and spread it on the table, full in the light of the tallows. 'Just before he was done in. Not a quarter of a minute!'

The Smith family stared at the document. None of them could read.

'What is it?' asked Miss Fanny.

''Twas what he was killed for,' said Smith, and went on to relate all the circumstances of the crime, not forgetting the unseen man with the limp, the thought of whom terrified him more than anything else.

'It's a deed to property,' declared Miss Bridget. 'For that queer thing' – she jabbed her needle at a piece of writing – 'that looks so like a horse and cart, is the word "property". Indeed it is. I'd know it anywhere!'

Smith was not convinced.

'Then why was he done in for it? And why was they so frantic when they couldn't find it? Poor old fool!'

'Reasons,' said Miss Bridget darkly and returned to the velveteen coat. 'Reasons.'

'*I* think,' said Miss Fanny, 'that it's a confession, or an accusation. For that's the sort of thing a murder's done for – excepting money; and it ain't money. Now – though I don't quarrel with Brid's "property", for I believe her to be right, there's a "whereas", most distinct; and that piece like a nest of maggots, there' – she pricked with her needle – 'I *know* to be "felonious". Oh yes indeed, Smut dear: you got a confession which will be very valuable if we can only find out what's been done. For, if they was willing and able to kill for it – well, they'll be equal willing to *pay* for it! Clever Smut!'

Smith frowned, still not convinced, but inclined more to a confession than a property deed. In his heart of hearts he thought the document might be something else altogether, but said nothing, having nothing to go on, nor any piece of knowledge to contradict his sisters with.

'So we must get it read out to us,' continued Miss Fanny, neglecting the breeches, 'so we can know where to apply.'

'And who, miss, would you ask?' queried Miss Bridget irritably.

'Lord Tom can read,' said Smith, thinking of his highwayman idol and friend.

'Lord Tom?' repeated Miss Fanny, blushing and smiling. 'The very scholar!'

Miss Bridget sneered. 'That high toby is so much in his cups, his mouth's grown like a spout! Mark my words, miss, I'd as soon trust him with anything worth money as I'd trust the landlord! Not that I think the paper's worth money at all: for it's neither more nor less than a deed to property.'

They went on arguing thus till the tallows burned low: with Miss Bridget inclining more and more to property, and Miss Fanny, who was softer and younger, being scarce nineteen, keeping to the romantic notion of a confession on whose value as blackmail they might all live happily ever after. But on one thing they were all agreed: the difficulty of finding anyone they could trust enough to read it to them.

At length, when the room was full of tallow smoke and shifting shadows, Miss Bridget and Miss Fanny retired to their curtained-off bedroom, and Smith to his corner in the workroom itself.

For some minutes one tallow remained alight,

and afforded Smith a sombre view of the brown velveteen coat and the grey breeches bespoken by the hangman. They were upon a hook in a corner and presented a disagreeable resemblance to their aspect when their last owner had last worn them. Smith wondered if he was likely to come back for them, fearfully white and moaning about the cold. Well – they'd not fit him now!

He screwed up his face scornfully at the thought of ghosts; but continued to stare into dark corners till he fell asleep, and, when he awoke, did so with a startled air and looked about him with some relief to see the old brick and plaster walls and the dim grey daylight falling down the cellar steps . . . as if his dreams had given him cause to doubt his firm belief in no ghosts.

The document was still on the table. He folded it up and began to tiptoe towards the stairs.

'Where are you off to, Smut dear?'

Miss Fanny, much tousled and creased, had poked her head through the curtain.

'Newgate,' said Smith, briefly. 'Got business.'

'What are you going to do with our dockiment, Smut?'

'Don't know – yet.'

'Wouldn't it be safer here?'

'Why?'

'Well, dear – if them that wanted it did in an old man for it, they won't think twice about doing in a boy.'

'Don't know I got it! Never saw me! There's only you and Miss Bridget what knows.'

'Oh yes . . . that's true. But you never can tell, Smut. *Someone* may have seen you. Won't you leave it behind?'

'No.'

'Are you going to show it to Lord Tom?'

'Don't know. Maybe.'

'If he's going to Newgate,' came Miss Bridget's voice, still croaked with sleep, 'tell him to screw some money out of that Mr Jones – for there'll not be another stitch done till there's something on account! Hangmen is horrible customers! So degrading!'

Miss Fanny's head, which had vanished for the moment, reappeared.

'Mr Jones, Smut. Brid says, see Mr Jones.' Then she sighed. 'For the last time, dear – leave the dockiment behind. 'Twill be safe as houses. Oh, Smut! I've an 'orrible feeling you was seen and are in danger! Oh, Smut! I fear you'll be coming down them steps tonight stone dead!'

Chapter 3

A tremendous idea had lodged in Smith's mind and, like all truly great things, answered its purpose so exactly that one exclaimed, 'Why hadn't it been thought of before?' He would *learn* to read!

The morning was dull and windy. The cathedral birds were huddled upon Old Bailey, which stood to the lee-ward side of the stench from Newgate Gaol. Such merchants and clerks and attorneys who walked the whipping streets kept their heads down and their hands to their wigs and hats – as if to hold their aspiring thoughts from flying out to become common property. A general frown and scowl creased their faces: another day was bad enough, without the insolent wind aggravating it!

Smith had spread the document inside his coat and across his chest, where it kept him from the worst of the weather.

'Be still, old fellow,' he muttered from time to time as the stiff paper pricked and tickled. 'You and me's got business. You and me's going up in the world . . . just as soon as I gets you to talk!'

He was crossing Ludgate Hill when suddenly he fancied he saw the murdered old gentleman, stumping along ahead of him. He stopped, much frightened. Then he looked again and saw that the old gentleman was someone else altogether. But thereafter the murdered man stayed pretty firmly in his thoughts – as if keeping a watch on his document and where Smith was taking it.

Which, in the first place, was to the blackened and gloomy felonage of Newgate Gaol. Smith turned in at the lodge, greeted the gaoler there, and lit up his battered pipe against the dreadful smells to come.

First, he found out Mr Jones, the hangman: a short, stout, horny-handed gent who shone with pomatum. He got three shillings out of him on account – together with a surly prophecy that if he, Smith, didn't mind his *P*'s and *Q*'s he'd become Mr Jones's customer in a transaction with a yardage of hemp.

'*P*'s and *Q*'s?' said Smith, earnestly. 'Them's letters, ain't they?'

Mr Jones agreed.

'Then show us a *P*, Mister Jones, and then show us a *Q*, and I'll try to mind 'em!'

For the thought had occurred to Smith that two letters would be a fair start to the day's work of learning to read. Unluckily, Mr Jones took him for a humorist and aimed a thump that would have been pleasurable if it had struck.

Bleeding scholars! thought Smith, as he scuttled out of the hangman's office. Want to keep everything to themselves!

From Mr Jones's, it was but a brief, though dark and sullen, way down a ragged stairway, along a passage, a turn to the right then up two steps, to the Stone Hall, where Smith's present hopes were most likely to be passing the time of what was neither night nor day. The Stone Hall was a long, low, arched room with its own stone sky and its own six lanterns for a sun. When these were lit, it was day, when they were out, it was night – no matter what the outside heavens were declaring.

Smith's present hopes shuffled somewhere among the lost multitude of the Town's rubbish and dregs. Grumbling rag-bags and tattered felons, debtors who always looked surprised and, here and there, like a fallen moon, a pale white face of unbroken pride – most likely of a man due to be hanged.

Here was Smith's place of daily business; for he ran errands for the debtors – twopence a mile dry, and fourpence when it rained.

Very educated gentlemen, the debtors. A man needs to be educated to get into debt. Scholars all. The first Smith tried was a tall, fine-looking gentleman who, though still in leg-irons, walked like he owned the gaol – as well he might, for his debts could have bought it entire.

He smiled; he was never at a loss for a smile . . . which was, perhaps, why he was there; when a man can't pay what he owes, a smile is a deal worse then nothing!

'Learn us to read, mister!' said Smith, humbly.

The fine debtor stopped, looked – and sighed.

'Not in ten thousand years, my boy!' and, before Smith could ask him why, he told him.

'Be happy that you can't! For what will you get

by it? You'll read and fret over disasters that might never touch you. You'll read hurtful letters that might have passed you by. You'll read warrants and summonses where you might have pleaded ignorance. You'll read of bills overdue and creditors' anger – where you might have ignored it all for another month! Don't learn to read, Smith! Oh! I implore you!'

Then the gentleman drifted, smiling, away, with his back straight, his head held high – and his ankles jingling.

Next, Smith applied to a learned felon, a ferret-faced man with small, starry eyes.

'What d'yer want to read for, Smith? No need. And if it weren't for me skill as a reader, I'd not be here today. I was on the run – and saw a new goldsmith's sign. Stopped to read it – and 'ere I am! No, stay ignorant, me boy – and keep out of 'arm's way.'

Smith pleaded – but the felon was determined, so Smith left him and would have gone from the Stone Hall had he not seen Mr Palmer.

This Mr Palmer was a debtor of a different sort: a gentle, sad man who could not bring himself to believe that the world had been so spiteful as to gaol him. (Even though it had been these past five years.) For Mr Palmer – did the world but know it – nourished a very high opinion of himself, which he was careful to hide for fear of its being damaged.

'Learn us to read, Mister Palmer!'

Mr Palmer stopped in mid-shuffle.

'Learn us to read, Mister Palmer!'

Mr Palmer turned on Smith a look of amazement that hid a powerful contempt and dislike – even loathing – for this debtor loathed, hated and despised every mortal thing that was better off than himself by being free.

'A pleasure to *"learn"* you, Smith,' he said. 'Here, boy.' He bent down and beckoned. Smith approached. 'This is how we begin!'

He seized Smith's nose as hard as he could and pulled and twisted and wrenched it till Smith's squeals filled the Stone Hall and his eyes fairly gushed with tears. Then his own voice was raised even louder, in a fearful bellow of pain. He'd forgotten Smith wore no leg-irons and could use his feet to advantage.

In an instant Smith was fled, leaving Mr Palmer with an empty finger and thumb, and a pair of shins that were splintered with booting. He lay on the ground and continued to roar, only breaking off to pray that the ungrateful brat who'd crippled him might come to a bad end on Mr Jones's rope; while Smith, full of anger and humiliation and a burning pain in his nose, left Newgate Gaol swearing a solemn oath that, not till he was took, would he ever set foot in that foul place again!

With his hands pressed to his chest and his eyes still streaming with forced tears, he ran towards the nestling of lanes about the great cathedral. Soft-hearted ladies stared as he passed, moved by the sight of the weeping urchin. Then his eyes dried up, his nose recovered – and his grand determination flared anew. He *would* learn to read! For he and the document were going up in the world – though the Devil himself stood against them!

Surely the Town had more scholars than those in Newgate Gaol? The streets must be full of them! He'd only to ask. No harm in asking . . . He crossed the windy street to meet with a round-faced old gentleman with an absent-minded air.

'Mister – mister! Learn me to read!'

The gentleman paused – momentarily taking his hand from his hat. In an instant the wind whipped it off, together with his wig, leaving him as bald as the dome of St Paul's. Smith, meaning no offence, began to grin. The gentleman raised his stick – and Smith fled for his life!

He asked a lawyer, a clerk, a country schoolmaster – but they'd have none of him. He poked his head through the window of a carriage waiting outside an apothecary's to ask of the elderly lady sat within. But she shrieked and shouted to her footman to frighten him off. At last, he found himself in Holborn Hill, passing by grey, high-shouldered St Andrew's Church. The Church: Mother of the Town – and all creatures in it!

With renewed hope he shuffled up to the porch and peered into the richly stained gloom of the church's insides. Blood of glass martyrs fell across the aisle and drenched the altar . . . and there was a smell of damp stone in the quiet air. A very peaceful, genteel sort of place.

At first, it seemed empty – and Smith had some brief thoughts concerning the candlesticks.

'What d'you want, my child?'

A priest was in the pulpit, still as a carven saint.

'Oh, it's beautiful!' said Smith, ingratiatingly. 'Just like me sisters' stories of heaven!'

The priest nodded and smiled kindly.

'What are you looking for, my child?'

'Guidance, Your Reverence,' said Smith, who'd decided, this time, to ask roundabout.

'Are you lost?'

'Oh no, Your Worship! This is 'olborn 'ill!'

The priest compressed his lips and eyed Smith shrewdly. Hurriedly, Smith went on, 'Learn me to read, Your 'oliness. That's what I come for. Learn me to read so's I can read the 'oly Scripture.'

The priest stared in amazement at the filthy, strong-smelling little creature who stood in the aisle with his black hands pressed to his grubby heart.

'If you come and stand by the door during Service, then you'll hear me reading from the Holy Scripture, child. Won't that be a comfort and help?'

'Oh yes, Your Grace. And I'm humbly obliged. But what of when I'm 'ome – all in dirt and disorder? Who'll read to me then? And me two poor sisters – a-panting, a-groaning, a-supplicating for salvation? Who'll read to them? Oh, no, Your Reverence – I got to learn to read so's I can comfort meself in the dark o' the night . . . and light a little lamp in me sisters' souls with perusings aloud from the Good Book!'

But this was too much.

'You're a little liar!' exclaimed the priest, abruptly. Smith gazed thoughtfully up at him, proud in his white surplice and bands.

'And you're a fat bag of rotting flour!' he snarled suddenly. 'I 'ope the weevils gets you!'

Was there no one in all the Town who'd teach Smith to read?

He passed the top of Godliman Street. A man came out from somewhere, stopped . . . and stared at him palely. But Smith, still disheartened by the church's rejection, did not see him and went wearily on.

Smith came to the booksellers in St Paul's Churchyard. A last hope for the day. And where better to learn to read than in a bookshop?

Several times he idled up and down, judging his chances in each shop. Here, a proprietor scowled at him; there, a clerk shook his fist . . . and there an entrance was blocked by a fat man who seemed to have died in the act of reading, but came to life to turn a page and acknowledge the helpless bookseller with a corpse-like nod.

But there was one shop that attracted Smith by the mad profusion and tottery architecture of its wares. Books stood in walls and towers and battlements, as if the owner had been in a state of siege for a hundred years – which was partly borne out by his appearance. He was an amazingly thin, wary little man with a nervous affliction which made his head dart from side to side as if wondering from where the attack might come. Nor was he put at ease when he saw Smith. For he'd seen Smith before – even knew him . . .

He sat in a curious kind of cave of books where he could jerk and twitch in privacy and quiet.

'Learn us to read, mister!'

'Be off with you!' he said curtly, jerking his head to the right.

'Ain't you got no feelings for yore trade?' asked Smith earnestly. 'Don't you want it to prosper with more readers –'

'– You're a wicked little thief!' said the bookseller, now jerking to the left.

'– Only because I'm ignorant!'

'Get out of here!'

'*Why* won't you learn me?'

'Keep your thieving hands to yourself!'

'Why won't anybody learn me?'

'Because they've too much sense –'

'– All this goodness and wisdom and learning –' Smith was grandly pointing to the dusty cliffs that reared on either side.

'Touch a book and I'll finish you!'

The bookseller was now jerking and twitching pretty vigorously and, as his head flew from side to side, Smith considerately tried to keep pace with it – which made him appear as if he was performing a wild dance.

'Keep still!' shouted the bookseller of a sudden – and jerked worse than ever.

Too late. Smith, capering wider and wider, struck first against one and then against the other of the two tottering shelves.

The calamity that followed, though of brief duration, was terrific in its scope. It was as if the long siege was at last over and the enemy had breached all the walls at once!

The two walls of shelves had collapsed and, with them, brought down in a mighty and thunderous torrent, every last item in the whole of the ramshackle shop!

Books in their fluttering and dusty thousands poured and thumped down as if the very skies had been loaded with them. Histories, Memoirs, Diaries, Lexicons, Grammars, Atlases, Journals, Biographies, Poems, Plays . . . books about heaven, books about hell, huge books about pygmies, tiny books about giants – even books about books – all, all slid and tumbled into a desperate ruin overhung by a bitter cloud of dust. And somewhere underneath it all, still jerking and twitching, though feebly now, lay the unlucky bookseller himself!

Gawd! thought Smith, half-way round the Cathedral and going like the wind, 'e must be squashed flatter than an old sixpence.

But the bookseller was alive, and, while Smith was still running and wondering hopelessly whom next he could ask to teach him to read, his last victim was being exhumed by neighbours and passers-by. Strangely enough he seemed almost the better for the disaster, as though, all his life, he'd expected and dreaded it and now that it had happened a load was fallen from his soul. He jerked and twitched hardly at all as he told how it had come about and who'd been chiefly to blame.

'They call him Smith,' he said.

'And where does he come from?'

'Somewhere near the Ditch. I fancy it's the Red Lion Tavern . . .'

The questioner had been a passer-by: the man who'd earlier come out of Godliman Street.

Chapter 4

At about five o'clock Smith went home, having spent every penny he had (except the three shillings he'd screwed out of Mr Jones) on meat pie, ale and tobacco. And, though there'd been pockets in plenty for the picking, he'd kept his hands to himself. For the first time he could remember he was frightened of being caught; for then he'd lose whatever might be the benefit of the document, which was still pressed against his chest, where it was growing strong with sweat.

*

'Hullo, Smith! Not nubbed yet?'

Deep in thought, he ignored the landlord's pleasantry and made for the cellar steps. From below the tallows gleamed yellowly and cast strange shadows on the wall. He began to descend, when –

'Stand and deliver!'

A voice like twelve o'clock of St Paul's roared from the heart of the cellar! Smith started, missed a step, and came down the rest any way but on his feet!

A dangerous, glittering, murdering adventurer of a gentleman in green stood before him, aiming a pistol the scope of a cannon directly at his head! It was his friend, Lord Tom, the high toby, come on a sociable visit.

'Do watch how you go, Smut,' cried Miss Fanny, 'or you'll be coming down them steps stone dead! And *then* where will our dockiment be?'

'Did you see that degrading Mr Jones?' asked Miss Bridget. 'For if you didn't you can go straight out again, broken pate or nothing!?'

'Pleased to see you, Lord Tom,' said Smith, picking himself up and rubbing his head. 'They told me you was nubbed – but I never believed 'em.'

'Ah!' said the highwayman, putting up his pistol and smiling sadly through his brackenish beard. 'It happens to all of us, sooner or later, Smut. With some, it's sooner; but with Lord Tom, let's hope it'll be vastly the later!'

'And so say all of us,' murmured Miss Fanny, as she might have said, Amen!

'Trade been good these past ten days, Lord Tom?' asked Smith, giving over the three shillings to Miss Bridget who hid them somewhere behind the curtain, away from the highwayman's quick green eyes.

'Been on the Finchley Common, Smut, me young friend. Wild and free on the snaffling lay!'

'Don't use them coarse expressions!' came Miss Bridget's voice. 'If you mean pilfering from unarmed travellers, then say so. Or are you ashamed?'

Lord Tom grinned at Smith (who grinned back) and then at Miss Fanny who sighed and blushed.

'Many coaches, Lord Tom? And was there danger?'

'Fine smart equipages, little Smut! Windows fair sparkling with satin and brilliants. Like travelling stars, I tell you. Gleaming in the foggy nights. It's a life, my boy! Stand and deliver! Stern with the gentry: courteous with the ladies. "Madam, your necklace – if you please! Sir, your purse – or I'll blow your head off!"'

'And did you, Lord Tom?' asked Smith, smiling wistfully at the thought of riding out with his friend – which had always been one of his dearest dreams. 'Did you blow any heads off this time?'

'Only a pair of coachmen's, Smut! And then unwillingly – for they went for their weapons.'

'How many coaches did you take?'

'Six, me friend! Six gay glitterers –'

'Then where's your profit, you ugly murderer!' came Miss Bridget's voice – for she'd refused to come out and join the company. 'Where's the necklaces and purses, sir?'

Lord Tom sighed. 'Spent, Miss Bridget – as well you know. That's the way of our lives. Risk all for the chase – then spend the profit in high contempt. The chase and the danger's all!' (Here, Smith nodded vigorously.) 'There was a diamond brooch I parted with for an evening's ale in Highgate, ma'am. And, by God, but it was a good exchange! Eat, drink and be merry, as they say – for tomorrow we'll all be nubbed!'

'A pity it wasn't yesterday!' snapped Miss Bridget and, for the first time, the highwayman looked angry. But it passed and he went on with his adventures, to Miss Fanny's admiration and Smith's envy and delight.

'But what's this I hear,' he said at length and, with his hands on his hips, high high-booted legs apart, surveyed Smith with an amiable smile. 'For the news I hear' – he nodded affectionately to Miss Fanny – 'is that *you've* come upon a rare treasure, me lad! Already me rival in accomplishment? Well, indeed – I'm proud of you! A document, I hear tell. And curiously valuable – from all accounts.'

'I told Lord Tom,' put in Miss Fanny, stopping her sewing with her needle at full stretch. 'And we're of an opinion that –'

'– 'Tis nothing of value!' said Miss Bridget, coming at last through the curtain, her handsome face much flushed. 'A property deed, most likely. Of no use to anyone at all!'

'And I say it's a confession, Brid! Reely, Lord Tom, dear – I'm convinced! Indeed, the more I think on it, it had such – such a *guilty* look!'

'Well, then,' exclaimed Lord Tom cheerfully, 'let's put an end to conjecture and see it. Here, Smut, old comrade-in-arms, let's see the document. Lord Tom'll read it for you.'

Smith, suddenly uneasy, stared at his two sisters, one frowning and the other softly open-mouthed.

Then he looked up at his friend, the glittering, dangerous highwayman. He hesitated . . . and began to back towards the stairs. Now that his secret was about to be revealed he felt unsure, even unwilling . . . For a whole day the document had been next to his heart. He felt strangely that he'd be betraying it if he gave it up now. He continued to look suspiciously from one to another of the company.

'Well, Smut, friend – where's the treasure?'

'I – I ain't got it, Lord Tom . . . I – I left it with a friend!'

'Not that creeping Mr Palmer?' exclaimed Miss Bridget. 'How I hate debtors! They're worse'n thieves!'

Smith shook his head and rubbed his nose ruefully.

'Then who's got it, Smut, dear? Who's got our valuable dockiment?'

'The parson in St Andrew's.'

'And who's he, when he's at home? You little liar!' said Miss Bridget coldly.

'A friend o' mine.'

'You made him up!'

'No, Miss Bridget! True as I live an' breathe. Big fat man all in white. Friend of mine. Cross my heart and hope to be nubbed!'

'And where did you meet him?'

'In church –'

'Now I *know* you're lying! For you never was in a church in all your born days! Liar and blasphemer! Oh, how I hate a liar! Nothing's more degrading! You come here – you young person – and I'll wash your mouth out with vinegar for you. Don't think you'll escape this time!'

Miss Bridget – who had indeed a jar of vinegar in her hand – began to advance on Smith with her eyes glinting venomously. Smith dodged briefly behind Lord Tom and hung on to the tops of his boots.

'Never come 'tween a family,' chuckled the highwayman – and stepped aside so's Smith stumbled and fell. Miss Bridget came on. Smith howled and fled behind Miss Fanny. Who obliged by crying, 'Poor Smut!' and flouncing aside to the stairs.

Smith began to dart round the cellar at so great a rate that the tallow flames tore after him as if to rip loose from their seatings.

'I'll teach you to lie to me!' shouted Miss Bridget, making strong dives at her brother who, between howling and roaring his innocence, kept dragging table and stools and every movable article into her path.

On the stair – cutting off all retreat – sat Miss Fanny and Lord Tom, laughing fit to burst.

'Let me through!' panted Smith, each time he passed.

'Not till you give up the document!' laughed Lord Tom.

'Oh, do as Lord Tom says, dear Smut,' cried Miss Fanny, 'before Brid mashes you stone dead! For she's that vexed.'

Smith shook his head and rushed on more fiercely than ever, for Miss Bridget, having the longer legs, was gaining . . . Round and round he scuttled and darted – now like a sooty moth – now like a quick black rat. And each time he passed the stair he begged and implored Miss Fanny and Lord Tom to make way for his desperate, panting self.

'Not till we see the document! Ha-ha! Not till you give up your treasure!'

While from behind, Miss Bridget panted grimly, 'Nothing'll save you this time! You degrading little liar, you!'

She made a last tremendous lunge – both to save herself (for she'd tripped on a stool) and to seize her brother's hair. Smith shrieked. Lord Tom laughed. Miss Fanny cried, 'Poor Smut!' when there was a fateful interruption: the landlord.

His greasy head hung over the stair like a dirty street lamp.

'Smith! Smith! Forgot to tell you something!'

Hastily, Miss Bridget let go of his hair and genteelly wiped her fingers.

'What?'

'You 'ad callers. Two.'

'Who? Me?'

'Yes, indeed. Had you off to a *T*. Dirty, weaselish, villainous-looking remnant. Eyes like chips of coal. Teeth like the same. About twelve year old. – "That's him!" I says directly. – "Good!" says they. "And where is he?" – "Nubbed, most likely," says I. – "Oh-ho!" says they, "we'll be back then – to inspect the remains." Then they was off. No message. Just that.'

'W-what was they like?'

'One tall: t'other short. Wearing brown. And, though I says it myself (and I ought to know), as unsavoury and throat-slittish a pair as ever I've clapped eyes on! Ha-ha!'

The landlord's head was hoisted out of view and there was a deep silence in the cellar. Smith shivered uncontrollably. He was desperately frightened. God knew how the two men in brown had tracked him down; but they had done so. He could not stop his teeth chattering. Even Miss Bridget looked at him compassionately.

'It – it's them!' he whispered. 'They've come to slit me throat!'

'Don't you worry, me lad!' exclaimed Lord Tom, grimly. 'There's no high toby, thief or rascal who'd dare come here when he knows Lord Tom's on your side! By God, Smut! If they so much as sets foot on them stairs, I'll blow blue daylight through the both of them! You've a man to protect you now. And I can't say fairer than that.'

'No,' muttered Smith. 'You don't know 'em. They're not your sort, Lord Tom –'

'Why, Smut! You'll be safe with Lord Tom! There, dear – you just give him our dockiment and all will be well.'

'You don't understand! They'll do for me anyways. They're that sort.'

'Then what will you do, child?' asked Miss Bridget, much troubled.

'I don't know . . . But I can't stay 'ere. Not now. Not at night! I'll go off somewhere. Maybe to –'

'– To the parson at St Andrew's?' smiled Lord Tom.

'Maybe . . .'

'Don't lie now, child. It may be for the last time . . . and you'd go to hell.'

Smith looked round the cellar which was his home, very mournfully and wretchedly. 'I got to go! For Gawd's sake, let me past!'

Lord Tom shrugged his shoulders, but stood aside. 'I'd protect you, Smut. Honest, I would.'

'The dockiment, Smut. Won't you leave it, dear? It'll bring you no good –'

'No!' said Smith, fiercely. 'Never! Never! Never!' He paused, as if shocked by his own determination, then added, 'Besides, it's with the parson at St Andrew's.'

'Oh, Smut,' sighed Miss Fanny. 'Brid's right – and you're a liar. For you got it inside of your coat. I can see it, dear.'

'Out o' my way!' shouted Smith – and, with a desperate rush, flew up the stairs and was gone.

Chapter 5

Two men – one short, the other tall – who might have been dressed in brown (the street was too dark to be sure), saw Smith hurry out of the Red Lion Tavern. They'd been in a doorway nearby. Deep in shadows. They did not think they'd been observed. After a few seconds they set off together in the wake of the hurrying boy. They followed him for about five minutes along the nearly empty Saffron Hill. Then they lost him. He seemed to have vanished into the gloomy air. Half a minute later he was seen – unexpectedly – on their left, at the corner of Cross Street, hurrying like a mad thing. They nodded and set off again.

This time they kept him in sight for nearly ten minutes; then he vanished near Cony Court. They waited a while, listening, for the narrow streets and alleys hereabouts were very quiet, and even a rat's scuttle would have been heard. Now they entered the shadowy confines of the court – were about three yards within it – when the boy was seen again, darting desperately back towards Cross Street, his alarmed eyes glittering in the light of some late merchant's window.

Back went the two followers, their shoulders hunched – for the night was growing bitterer by the minute – and their feet kissing the cobbles with a grim, urgent passion. They did not let him out of their sight for more than an instant. Portpool Lane – Hatton Garden – Chart Street – back into Saffron Hill, then Holborn Hill – Union Court – Hatton Garden again – and so to Cross Street – Saffron Hill – Cox's Court . . .

An intricate necklace of flight was being threaded as the three hurrying figures shifted through and round the lanes, courts and alleys that lay, ragged and near deserted, under a gnawed rind of the moon.

Sometimes there was not above five yards between them; and then they'd lose him for a few seconds – oddly, unaccountably – like he'd gone up in a puff of black smoke ... Till there he'd be again, come suddenly from some dark passageway of which nothing had been seen till then.

There seemed to be many dozens of these crevices in the black, lumpy substance of the frowning houses – but, sooner or later, there'd be one whose end would be sewn up tight as a sock: a fatal passage from which there'd be no panting scuttle of escape.

The boy had left the Red Lion Tavern at half after six by St Paul's. At a quarter to nine o'clock, the followers leaned up against a wall in Hatton Garden.

Breathed one: 'Fer God's sake! I can't go another step! Me heart'll burst – I swear it!'

Came a low reply, much charged with pain and phlegm: 'All right! We'll go back – some'ow – to the Red Lion. We'll wait there ... God rot the crafty little perisher!'

With painful steps they limped away, so

wind-broken by two and a quarter hours of unceasing pursuit that they seemed scarce able to drag their own meagre shadows down the cold street.

Ten minutes later, in a narrow abutment no more than a yard from where they'd been leaning, a shadow moved. Then a face edged out: a small, pointed, wary face. It surveyed the empty street. It grinned – not with pleasure, but with a savage and desperate triumph. Smith had done what he'd set out to do when he'd seen the men waiting for him as he'd left the Red Lion. He'd run his pursuers into the ground.

He began to walk – somewhat slowly, for his own sides were aching villainously. Presently, he stopped and drew the sweat-drenched document from under his coat. He studied it by the thin, cold light of the moon. It did not seem much the worse for its wetting. Miss Bridget's 'property' and Miss Fanny's 'felonious' looked as much like a horse and cart and a nest of maggots as ever. None the less, at the first opportunity, he picked a passing pocket of a handkerchief and wrapped the document up. Then he sighed with relief and set off for another part of the Town.

*

Though no one followed him now, he moved with extraordinary circumspection; for the dark houses and the dimly silvered streets held another, more formidable menace. Time and again he fancied he heard other footsteps – steps that limped awkwardly – and he thought of the unseen lame man with the soft voice.

But these alarms were in his mind alone and, if they ever came to anything, they never turned into more than the totterings of some drunken home-goer, or the limping of a chairman, weary unto death and cursing under his breath.

Now he was in High Holborn, and the tall buildings on either side scowled blackly down with, here and there through an ill-drawn drape, a yellow sneer of light; while ceaselessly down the wide street, like the Devil's own crossings' sweeper, came a bitter wind, whipping up the Town's rubbish into spiteful ghosts of dust and paper that plucked and nipped and stung the living boy.

His nose, chin and fingers were beginning to burn with the cold. Not a night to be out in: black and windy, with the moon now doused in a creeping sea of cloud. He passed by a gloomy ale-house with a bunch of iron grapes groaning from its sign. He stopped – fingered a guinea he'd got with the handkerchief – and thought of a bed for the night.

But the house was full, so he took a half a pint of gin to keep out the cold, the loneliness and the shifting fear – to no purpose. The gin sickened him and inflamed his brain so's he heard everywhere the soft voice he dreaded and the awkward scrape of a leg, quaintly lame. He began to search for the door – and was helped by a pair of potboys who came at him, slantwise, from somewhere in the smoky room.

Out again into the bitter street. Above his head the iron grapes creaked menacingly, back and forth – back and forth . . . He moved away, fearful that they'd drop and crack him like an egg.

But it was not the grapes alone; the very houses seemed to be shuddering against the blotched sky. He shifted out into the middle of the street, for he'd a sudden horror that all the buildings were tottering in upon him. The sky seemed to grow smaller and smaller and the jagged roofs, fanged with chimneys, seemed to snarl and snap as if to gobble him up.

He began to run, wildly: now from side to side of the street, banging into posts, stumbling across the gutter, turning down lanes and alleys that were new even to him ... And all this with a curious, hopeless urgency: his feet running like a hanged man's feet – seeming to reach for a purchase on a world that was slipping away.

Where was he going? God knew! Maybe even in search of the two men in brown to give up the document. For suddenly it seemed to him that the document was a fearful disease that was burning and poisoning him – after tempting him madly from the shelter of his home.

At last he found himself in a long, wide street, where the moon had widowed all the houses, with black hatchments under their porches ... Vaguely, he thought he knew where he was. There was a narrow turning any minute now ... an alleyway that would lead him, deviously, back to the Red Lion. He fancied he saw it. He turned –

'Watch out! Watch out! Oh! Oh! Ah!'

At the very moment Smith had turned into the alley a gentleman had come out of it. They met and, though the gentleman was tall and stout and huge beside Smith, he was struck with such speed and force that he fell with an angry frightened cry.

Smith struggled to his feet, was about to rush on, when a hand grasped at his ankle.

'Let go!' he shouted.

'Damn you, no! Help me, first –'

Smith glared wildly down. He saw the gentleman's face, grey as a puddle. His eyes were sunken and dark: no spark of light in them.

'Help me up! Help me, I say! For pity's sake, sir! Can't you see I'm blind?'

'A blind man!' gasped Smith. 'Oh Gawd! A mole-in-the-hole!'

The gin's tempest dropped abruptly away and left a glum wreckage behind, bleak and forlorn in the freezing night.

A boy – a child, thought the blind man, uneasily. Most likely a young thief. Most likely he'll rob me and run off – frightened out of his miserable wits. Oh God! How am I to get home?

'If you let go me ankle,' muttered Smith, 'I'll help you up; that's if you're really blind. Can you see me?'

The gentleman shook his head.

'What am I doing now?' asked Smith, pulling a hideous face.

'I don't know – I don't know! I swear I'm blind! Look at my eyes! Any light in 'em? Look for my smoked spectacles. They're somewhere about. Look for –'

'What am I doing now?' demanded Smith

pulling another, even more monstrous face; for he'd help no one who didn't need it.

The blind man loosed his hold on Smith's ankle and heaved himself up on one elbow. He'd lost his hat and his wig was awry, but otherwise he'd suffered no harm. He began to feel the adjacent cobbles for his possessions. Smith watched him and his face returned to normal, but as a last measure he fished inside his coat and pulled out the document.

'What have I got in me hand?' he asked gruffly.

The blind man sighed. 'My life, my boy . . . my life's in your hand.'

Smith scowled and put away the document. 'Here you are, Mister Mole-in-the-hole! Here's me 'and, then! Up with you! Up on yer pins! And 'ere's your 'at and stick and black spectacles . . . though why you wears 'em foxes me! My, but you're a real giant of a gent! Did you know it?'

This last as the blind man stood up and fairly towered over the helpful Smith.

'Thank you, boy. Now – tell me if I'm in the street or the alley and I'll give you a guinea for your pains.'

'You're on the corner.'

'Facing which way?'

'The Lord knows! I've been sick meself.'

'Fever?'

'Half a pint o' gin.'

Suddenly, Smith felt a strong desire to confide in the blind man. After all – it could do no harm.

'Smith,' he said, and held out one hand to be shook while with the other he guided the blind man's hand to meet it. 'Smith. 'Unted, 'ounded, 'omeless and part gin-sodden. Smith. Twelve years old. That's me. Very small, but wiry, as they say. Dark 'aired and lately residing in the Red Lion Tavern off Saffron 'ill. Smith.'

Helplessly, the blind man smiled . . . and his questing hand grasped Smith's firmly.

'Mansfield,' he said. 'Blind as a wall for these past twelve years. Well-to-do – but not much enjoying it. Mansfield. Residing at Number Seven Vine Street under the care of a daughter. Mansfield. Believe it or not – a magistrate!'

'Gawd!' gasped Smith. 'Oo'd 'ave thought I'd ever be shaking 'ands with a bleeding Justice?'

If Mr Mansfield heard he was too gentlemanly to remark on it. Instead, he fumbled in his coat for the promised guinea.

'And now, just point me toward the church that should stand at one end of the street and the guinea's yours, Smith, with my deepest thanks.'

Smith obliged – and took the guinea.

'Seems a lot for a little,' he said.

'Good night, Smith.'

'Same to you, Mister Mansfield, J.P.'

He watched the blind man tap his way down the street, bumping, here and there, into the posts – and sometimes raising his hat to them and mumbling, 'Sorry, good sir . . . couldn't see you . . . so sorry.'

Smith smiled indulgently and was about to make off, when a strangely familiar feeling of pity stirred in him. He had been reminded of the murdered old gentleman. He scowled at his own indecision, stuck his ancient pipe defiantly in his mouth, and hastened in the blind man's wake.

'That you, Smith?'

Smith grunted.

'Didn't expect you –'

'Going the same way meself.'

'To Vine Street?'

'Thereabouts.'

'Glad to hear it, Smith.'

Smith grunted again. 'Oh well – 'ere's me 'and, then . . . you old blind Justice, you! Just tell me where to turn and where to cross and I'll see you 'ome safe an' sound. After all – I ain't done much for that guinea.'

Mr Mansfield found the offered hand and, once more, grasped it. He sighed and reflected in his heart (which was far from being as blind as his eyes) that it was an uncanny thing to be the cause of kindness in others.

Vine Street lay about twenty minutes away. Mr Mansfield had strolled far that night, having a trouble-some problem that gnawed at him. But now, holding Smith's thin hand, the problem sank somewhat.

'Were it a sickness?' asked Smith after a while.

'My blindness, d'you mean? No. Lost my sight when a house burned down. Lost my wife as well. A costly fire, that!'

'Oh.'

'Take the next turning on the left, Smith.'

'What's it like – being blind?'

'Dark, Smith. Very dark. What's it like having eyes?'

'The moon's gone in again – so we're two of a kind, Mister Mansfield, you an' me.'

The blind magistrate felt somewhat taken down – but was cautious not to show it. Twelve years of his misfortune had taught him that a bland face was the best security for one in his situation and that, for a blind man to frown, scowl or laugh, even, was like a fool discharging his pistol wildly in the night. The Lord knew who'd be hit by it.

'If you can see a new-built church with a round tower, cross in front of it and walk with it to your right.'

Smith obliged. Hand in hand they passed by the church – a very curious pair indeed: small Smith, half a pace ahead, and huge, stout Mr Mansfield walking somewhat sideways and behind – for Smith tended to pull, rather.

'Vine Street is the next street that crosses this one. My house is to the right. I'll be safe enough now, Smith.'

'No trouble. I'm going the same way. To the door, Mister Mansfield.'

They came to Vine Street. Said Mr Mansfield: 'If you've naught better to do, will you come in and take a bite of late supper with me, Smith?'

'Don't mind if I do, Mister Mansfield.'

'Care to stay the night, Smith?'

'Don't mind if I do, Mister Mansfield.'

'Any family, Smith?'

'Sisters. Two of 'em.'

'Likely to worry?'

'Not much.'

'Then it's settled?'

'Just as you say, Mister Mansfield.'

'Anything else I can do for you, Smith?'

Smith sighed ruefully. The only thing he really wanted, Mr Mansfield was unable to provide.

'No, thank you, Mister Mansfield. You done all you can.'

They came towards the door of Number Seven. In spite of himself Smith grinned at the irony of his situation. Of all the men in the Town to bump into and befriend, he'd lit on the one who was blind and so could never teach him to read!

Chapter 6

Though she was amiable, charitable and kind to a degree, no one with a pair of eyes in his head would have mistaken her for a saint. She was made of a commoner humanity than that, and took full advantage of her father's blindness to scowl and grimace – and sometimes shake her small, fierce fist – when the blind man's disability caused her irritation or annoyance: which it often did. Thus, when Mr Mansfield blundered and broke some precious piece of porcelain, she'd cast her eyes to the ceiling with a look of phenomenal rage, but declare: ''Twas only a chipped cup, sir! I promise you, I'm glad it's gone! Come, sir, let me help you.' And her voice was always gentle and kind.

For all of twelve years this outward show of her human feelings, unseen by her father, had somehow created within a disposition of rare excellence, so that, at one and twenty she stood – not very tall but of great consequence – the most kindly but peevish and altogether remarkable young woman in the length and breadth of Vine Street.

Miss Mansfield stood on the topmost step, full in the light of the porch lamp. Below her waited a footman, ready to help his master.

'Papa!' she cried warmly. 'I was so worried! You've been gone so long, sir! I thought you was –'

Here she paused as Smith came into the light and she saw – what the blind man could not – that Smith was the filthiest, wretchedest and nearly the most sinister-looking object in the Town. '– lost,' she finished up, and her face expressed wonderfully her opinion of Smith.

Smith tugged at Mr Mansfield's hand, for he feared Miss Mansfield would set the footman on to do him a mischief.

'Daughter,' said the blind man. 'Here's Smith.

As good-hearted a child as the Town can boast of.'

Miss Mansfield did not look as though she believed it. Her face said very clearly: So. You've deceived him! Very well, then. You won't deceive me! *I've* a pair of eyes in my head! But aloud, she said: 'Pleased to make your acquaintance, Smith. Any friend of my father's is more than welcome.'

'Daughter,' said Mr Mansfield, mounting the steps and pulling Smith after him, 'my young friend's taking supper with us, and then he'll stay the night. For it's very bitter in the air and he's far from home.'

At this, Miss Mansfield looked so little pleased that Smith was amazed that even the blind man couldn't see it.

'Any friend of ours, sir –' she repeated, and bustled back into the house to attend to her father's wish.

They took supper in a back parlour – as clean, spacious and handsome a room as Smith had ever dreamed of, furnished with mahogany and with much neat silver on display. There were pictures on the walls and a fire in the grate, and it was a shame the blind man could see none of it, for a deal of trouble seemed to have been taken.

While they ate Miss Mansfield came and went some dozen times, with amiable inquiries or amusing observations (she was very talkative and spoke rather quick), but always with a look of the sharpest suspicion at Smith followed by a glance round the room to see what had been stolen. (I know what you're up to, her angry face said. But you'll not succeed. Not while *I've* a pair of eyes in my head!)

'A saint,' remarked Mr Mansfield once, when he was assured his daughter was gone from the room.

'Oh,' said Smith.

'You don't meet with a saint every day, Smith!' said Mr Mansfield, sounding somewhat offended by the cool response.

'No. You don't.'

Just then the saint came in to say Smith's bed was ready in a small room at the top of the house – and to shoot him as venomous and disgusted a look as ever he'd received in his life. He shivered, for he found his haven for the night uncanny . . . what with the blind Justice and the daughter at odds with herself.

None the less, he was, at bottom, an affable soul, and continued to talk with Mr Mansfield a while longer. He talked about life in the streets of the Town, life in the Red Lion's cellar, life in Newgate Gaol, death at Tyburn, and – death in Curtis Court. Yes, indeed, Smith mentioned – almost in passing – the happening that had turned him upside down and inside out.

'Indeed, I heard of it,' said the magistrate gravely. 'For the gentleman was known and wealthy.'

'Poor old so-and-so!' said Smith.

'Did you see him, then?'

'No!' said Smith, quickly; for how could he have known which was the old gentleman unless he'd seen him murdered? And if he'd seen that unlawful act, why hadn't he come forward?

Yes, indeed, Smith knew the law. And he suspected that the magistrate knew it even better.

'No, I never saw 'im. But I 'eard about it. Poor old so-and-so!'

Even as he spoke, some movement in the air – most likely due to their voices – caused the sideboard candle to flicker and jump and glint ironically in the blind man's dark spectacles . . . and a shadow was cast upon the opposing wall, strangely like the shape of the murdered old gentleman come quietly into the room to reproach Smith for denying him and to see what was becoming of his document.

'A Mr Field of Prickler's Hill in Hertfordshire. I knew him, Smith. A good but sad old gentleman. I'd like to have his murderer before me.'

'And so would I, Mister Mansfield!' muttered Smith sombrely, for he remembered well the old gentleman's look as the knife had gone in. 'Why was 'e done in?'

'I don't know, Smith; I don't know. But it's a vile, dark business . . .'

Mr Mansfield's ordinarily bland face grew hard and grim.

'It troubles me,' he murmured, more to himself than to Smith.

'What troubles you, Mister Mansfield?'

'My blindness. Because I shall never clap eyes on that murderer. Because, till the day I die, I'll never know what such a monster looks like. D'you understand me, Smith? D'you understand that, to me, devils and angels are all one?'

Smith did not entirely understand the blind man's strange sorrow; maybe because his mind was filled with the news that Mr Field had been wealthy. Hopes of the document were now very high.

'D'you understand me, Smith?'

Smith nodded, then recollected Mr Mansfield

couldn't see him and said, 'Yes, indeed!' and went on thinking of his prospects.

Soon after this Miss Mansfield came into the room and declared that it was growing too late to be talking.

'Not so much for you, Papa, but for your young friend. Truly, he looks tired, sir! His bed is ready – and he ought to be in it.'

Which remark, delivered most affably, was accompanied by a casting of eyes to the ceiling which said very plain: And the sheets he sleeps in will have to be burned! Oh, Papa! This is outrageous!

Smith's room was small and oddly shaped, owing to its situation under the roof. It was as though the builder, arriving nearly at the summit of his labour, had come upon this extra space by surprise and, on the spur of the moment, had popped a door and a window to it so's not to embarrass the stairs with leading to nowhere. A bed, a chest and a chair were the sole furnishings – and a pot of strong sweet herbs. For, though Miss Mansfield could burn the sheets after Smith had slept in them, she could not burn the room, so the herbs were the next best thing.

Now Smith, though he'd slept on straw all his life, wasn't so ignorant as not to know a bed when he saw one. He prodded it; he sat on it; he lay on it; he lay in it. He grinned – and directly went to sleep. This had not been his intention. He'd meant to have a great brood on his curious situation and enriched hopes. But the day had been too long for him, and the night too fierce. He was tired almost unto death. He slept without dreaming, without moving . . . He slept so long and so deep that Miss Mansfield, poking her head round the door in the morning, thought for an instant that he'd perished in the night and left behind him a small, black corpse.

'Smith!' she cried. 'Boy! Wake up! Directly!' And she poked at him with a walking stick she seemed to have brought especially for the purpose.

Smith woke up, saw Miss Mansfield's ferocious concern – and rolled deftly away. But he forgot he was sleeping two feet off the floor. He fell, and swore.

'Language!' shrieked Miss Mansfield and poked at Smith furiously with the stick. He howled.

'What's wrong?' Mr Mansfield cried from below.

'Nothing, Papa! Your young friend fell out of bed. Ha-ha! No harm done!'

Smith, unable to reach the door, had bolted under the bed. And there he crouched, very like a mouse, staring at Miss Mansfield's neat ankles and brisk, black shoes.

'Come out!' she muttered, and down flew her head, with her braided hair falling bolt downward to the floor like a pair of handsomely turned table-legs. 'No one's going to harm you!' And she prodded him with her stick to prove it.

'Are you here, daughter?'

Came a second pair of feet, large and slippered. Miss Mansfield's head – with a last furious scowl – vanished.

'Papa! You shouldn't have come without help! You might have fallen, sir!'

Mr Mansfield laughed. Miss Mansfield's feet shifted impatiently. The point of her stick kept prodding her toes – as if in default of another target.

'Morning, Smith. Sleep well? My daughter has a fine breakfast for you. She's a saint, child! As I told you – a real saint!'

Down came the saint's head. Come out! said her angry eyes. Come out, you disgusting object! Up went her head and vanished from view.

'Mornin', Mister Mansfield.' Smith had no quarrel with the blind man.

'What? Back in bed?' The slippered feet moved towards him. 'The voice betrays you! Give me your hand . . .'

Miss Mansfield's head was back again, peering round her father's ankles. Her lips moved. '*Please* come out!' Sourly triumphant, Smith shook his head.

'Where's your hand, Smith?' Mr Mansfield's voice – puzzled.

Miss Mansfield's eyes were filled with tears! (I beg you – for pity's sake, boy! Don't shame me in his blind eyes.)

Bewildered, Smith stared back. The mouse had made a discovery. The cat was as frightened and lost and lonely as he. Which was no comfort at all. Gloomily, he came out.

'Here's me hand, then . . . you old blind Justice, you!'

Over breakfast, which was taken in the back parlour, Mr Mansfield said: 'And will you go back to your cellar, Smith?'

Smith shrugged his thin shoulders. Miss Mansfield looked at him – and then to her father in weary aggravation. Did the blind man live but to spite her? What was he thinking of? So why didn't he come out with it, then? Must *everything* be left to her?'

'Smith,' she said, affecting a careless, everyday tone not reflected in her face, 'Mr Mansfield means, will you stay here? And work for your board and keep, of course! Mr Mansfield is very concerned about you. He thinks you deserve better of the world than you've got, and would give it to you. My father is quite a saint, you know –'

'Come, daughter! 'Tis your own idea.'

'Never! Never in ten thousand years! I read it all in your face, sir.'

'My face?'

''Tis like an open book to me.'

Smith, his mouth full, looked from one to the other of the Mansfields, each accusing the other of a kindness. He shrugged his shoulders. They might quarrel about it till the end of time. It would make no difference. He wasn't going to stay in that uncanny house. No, sir! Nothing on earth would have kept him with the Mansfields – blind father and mad daughter.

'Then it's settled,' said Miss Mansfield, with another irritated look at her father. 'Mr Mansfield will employ you in the stables, Smith . . . and I –' (Here, she looked: God help me!) '– will attend to your improvement. For a beginning, Smith, I shall teach you to read!'

Smith stared. He gaped. He poked his finger in his ear and scraped it about. What was it she'd said? Teach him to read? *To read*! He beamed . . . and beamed! He couldn't stop himself. He wondered if his face would ever go back again.

'I think he's pleased, Papa,' murmured Miss Mansfield in a low voice. 'I suppose he's fond of horses.'

Mr Mansfield offered to send a servant to the Red Lion to acquaint Miss Fanny and Miss Bridget with their brother's situation. But Smith said he'd rather go himself. The last thing he wanted was his improvement boasted of in the Red Lion's cellar! For, though he loved and trusted his sisters, he feared that, under such tortures as the two men in brown might inflict (such as the sight of five shillings – or even four), they'd wag their tongues like a pair of windy flags. 'Smut's in Vine Street! Poor little Smut!'

'I'll tell 'em tomorrow,' he said, and left it at that.

Now all was settled indeed, and Smith – on Miss Mansfield's orders – returned to his mad-shaped room. In high good humour he fell upon the bed and took out the precious document – the last remains of Mr Field of Prickler's Hill in Hertfordshire. Excitedly, he waved it aloft like a banner.

'Won't be long now, old fellow! Very soon you and me will be better acquainted! And then – up we'll go in the world!'

He folded it and wrapped it once more in the pilfered handkerchief. And not a moment too soon! Footsteps. Quickly, he pushed it into the tumbled bed linen. The door opened. Two footmen with real hangmen's faces. Alarm seized Smith. Why had they come? And why so grim?

'Up with you!' said one.

'And then down with you!' said the other.

'W-what d'you mean?'

They grinned. 'Miss's instructions. She says, afore you commence on scrubbing the yard, the self-same necessary thing must be done to you! So down to the scullery, young Smith!'

Smith's eyes glittered in alarm. Most likely he paled, too . . . but that wasn't so easy to see. He looked about him. But there was no escape. He looked up to the footmen. No mercy, nor even pity, there.

'To the scullery, young Smith.'

Now Smith had never been washed since, most likely, the midwife had obliged, twelve darkening years ago. Consequently, he suspected the task would be long, hard and painful. He was not mistaken.

Two more footmen, aproned over their livery, stood ready and waiting by a steaming iron tub.

'Take off them wretched rags, Smith.'

'Rags? What rags?' (The scullery was grey and stony and full of strong vapours.)

'Your clothes, Smith. Take off your clothes.'

The window was barred and the door was shut. He began to undress. Disdainfully, the footmen watched him; and indignantly, he stared back.

'Ain't you never seen a person take off his clothes before?'

Disdain gave way to amusement ... and then to surprise. Several times the footmen reached forward to seize him, for they thought he'd finished, but each time he waved them back.

''Ave the goodness to wait till I'm done, gen'lemen! 'Ave the goodness!'

For Smith wore a great many clothes. Indeed, to the best of anyone's knowledge, he'd never thrown a single item away. Coats and waistcoats worn to nothing but armlets and thread now came off him, and shirts down to wisps of mournful lace: one by one, removed carefully and with dignity, then dropped, gossamer-like, to the floor.

Then there were breeches consisting in nothing more than the ghosts of button-holes, and breeches that came off in greasy strips – like over-cured slices of ham; and breeches underneath that were no more than a memory of worsted, printed on his lean, sharp bottom.

These memories of perished clothes were everywhere, and plainest of all on his chest, where there was so exact an imprint of ancient linen that Smith himself was deceived – and made to take off his skin!

At last he crouched, naked as a charred twig, quivering and twitching as if the air was full of tickling feathers.

'Ready,' he said, in a low, uneasy voice, and the four footmen set to work.

Two held him in the tub; one scrubbed, and one acted as ladle-man. This last task was on account of the water having been dosed with sulphur, and it consisted in spooning off Smith's livestock as it rushed to the surface in a speckled throng.

From beginning to end, the washing of Smith took close upon three hours, with the scullery so filled with sulphurous steam that the footmen's misted faces grew red as the copper saucepans that hung like midnight suns on the scullery's streaming walls.

At last it was done. He was taken out, rinsed, and wrapped in a sheet – the ghost of his former self. For he was now a stark white replica of the previous Smith and, had his sisters seen him, they'd have shrieked and sworn it was his spectral image!

His clothes were burned before his oddly saddened eyes . . . which eyes were now seen to be somewhat larger and rounder than might have been supposed. But his hair, in spite of shock and scrubbing, remained as black as the river at night.

'Me clothes,' he said. 'Me belongings. I can't go about like this.'

Then he was told a livery was being cut down for him, and he was to go back to his room and wait. He mounted the stairs, much hampered by the sheet he was wrapped in. But there was great determination in him. Each fresh disaster he endured seemed to strengthen his bond with the document . . . and whatever it might contain. In a way, it seemed to be payment in advance.

He opened the door to his room. He stared. His eyes filled with tears of horror and dismay. The bed was stripped. The bedding was gone. And with it – the document!

Chapter 7

When they brought him his fine new livery (blue, with brass buttons), they wondered why he was sat, crouched on his bare bed, with his knees drawn up like battlements before his face. And they remarked, when they left him, on the look in his eyes as he watched them come and go: dismay and despair. They laughed on the way downstairs – but not unkindly – and decided his system was still shocked from his washing.

'Give him another half hour and he'll be trying

on his new clothes and strutting like the king of the weasels!'

But after half an hour there was no change, save that, maybe, Smith's head was sunk a little lower and his eyes stared with a deeper despair. His livery was untouched and the sheet that covered him had slipped an inch or two off his shoulders, leaving those thin objects to fend for themselves against the cold air.

'Maybe he's taken a chill?' suggested the housekeeper, and rummaged in her wits for a remedy.

'But he ain't flushed or feverish. He looks more froze than inly heated.'

Miss Mansfield came to see him. She scowled angrily at his sick, despairing air.

'Are you ill, Smith? What's wrong with you? Answer me!'

'Nothing, miss. Nothing.'

She went away, much troubled, and ordered blankets to be taken up – and Smith to be wrapped inside them.

Several times during the afternoon she returned, hoping against hope to find him restored. But each time he seemed more sunk within himself – as if something necessary had perished inside, and all was sinking inwards for lack of support. She questioned the four footmen and consulted with the housekeeper who gave it as her opinion that the child had been poisoned by too much sulphur and offered to prepare a draught. Gladly Miss Mansfield agreed. The draught was mixed and carried upstairs.

'Come, Smith. This will make you well again!'

But it was no use. He'd take neither draught nor anything else to sustain him.

'It's as if,' said the housekeeper quietly, 'that poor mite has made up his mind to die.'

'What an idea!'

'Scowl and frown as you please, miss, but I've seen it happen. These little souls of the Town perish like you and I go to sleep.'

And so it began to seem to all the Vine Street household save Mr Mansfield himself, from whom it was desperately kept – as was the late visit of a physician, brought in against all dignity through the tradesman's door with much secrecy and quiet.

He studied Smith. Felt his head, his wrist, his chest. Bade Smith look this way, that way, and to a point above his head. Wearily, Smith obliged, and everywhere his eyes turned they seemed to see even more misery – as if there was no end, no bottom to it. The physician shook his head. In all justice he could find nothing wrong; but in all compassion and pity there was something grievously amiss. But it was out of his scope to find it. He spread his hands, pocketed his fee, and left.

More and more Miss Mansfield blamed herself; had not the child been bright and well before his violent washing? But to her father's repeated inquiries she answered cheerfully: 'He's quite worn out from the footmen's labour, sir. I fancy he'll sleep the clock round. Best not disturb him yet.'

During the evening, Mr Billing called. Mr Billing was a youngish attorney and was both Mr Mansfield's friend and also deeply in love with his daughter. Mr Mansfield had high hopes of a marriage but he feared his daughter would never leave Vine Street as long as he lived. She always laughed when he brought the matter up and declared that Mr Billing was so agreeable a suitor that it would be a shame to bury him in a husband! Mr Mansfield would have dearly liked to have seen his daughter's face when she spoke so lightly . . . if only to see if her eyes were filled with regretful tears.

But on this evening Miss Mansfield found the attorney tiresome and overstaying his welcome; she longed to creep up to the top of the house and see the strange, sad child. She had a terrible feeling he'd die in the night.

Mr Billing stayed and stayed, affable and talkative as ever . . . and all the while she longed to cry out: 'Begone! Begone! There's a dying boy upstairs, and I must go to him.'

Instead, she helped him to port and brandy (as her father directed), and never left the room for an instant, being afraid of arousing her father's suspicions that all was not well with Smith. She chattered as amiably as she was able – and hoped her suitor would read the anxious impatience in her eyes. But, unluckily, Mr Billing was used to Miss Mansfield's varied and odd expressions and, though he loved each and all of them, he took no particular note of any.

Below stairs, all but two of the servants had gone to bed: a dozing footman and a certain scullery maid called Meg – a soft-hearted person with large arms the colour of boiled lobsters.

All the evening her muddled, motherly mind had been fixed on the sick child at the top of the house and a certain notion had come to her. Knowing that the boy had been brought up in an ale cellar she supposed he was homesick for all familiar things.

She brooded on this till there was no one about to question her, then she crept up to Smith with a pint of ale.

Not that she supposed he'd drink it, but she firmly believed that the sight and smell of it would do his aching heart a power of good.

Smith stared up at her mournfully. Her heart was fairly wrung. She moved about the tiny room to spread the ale's odours. Smith watched her. She smiled and held out the tankard.

'Come along, little one. It'll do you a power of good. Drink it up – for not the Red Lion itself has a better ale!'

Smith gazed at her sombrely.

'Nothing but kindness is meant. All's for your own good! They'll feed an' clothe you an' treat you like a yewmanbeen. You'll want for naught, here!'

Smith looked as though all he ever wanted was to pass, unhindered, away. Meg's eyes grew great with tears.

'They 'ad to wash you! You was that black! You should have seen the sheets –'

'The sheets? Did you see 'em?'

For the first time Smith showed signs of interest in the world. His nose twitched and his eyes began to kindle.

The ale, thought Meg triumphantly. It's the smell o' the ale what's doing it!

'Why, bless you, yes! And they was that horrible Miss wanted 'em burned!'

'And – did you?'

'Lor' no! Burn good sheets? I biled 'em!'

At this, Smith stared at her so strangely that she began to fidget.

'W-was there anything – anything else w-with the sheets?'

Obligingly, Meg shut her eyes to recall the scene.

'There was a handkerchief . . . but 'twas so far gone, I burned it –'

'Burned it?'

Here Smith gave such a shriek and a groan that Meg thought his last moment was come.

'I 'ad to, little one! 'Twas in a shameful state. It smelled, dear, like . . . well, I don't know what it smelled like, for I've naught to compare it with! Powerful. Clinging. I only 'ope it'll wear off the master's paper –'

'Paper?' whispered Smith, not daring to hope – and yet not able to prevent it. 'What – paper?' His eyes glittered so brilliantly, and he began to shiver so violently, that Meg edged away, fearing a contagious, mortal fever.

'Why – one of the master's documents that had somehow got itself muddled up in that dreadful 'andkerchief. Sometimes he drops 'is papers in the queerest places . . . what with his disability –'

'What was in it?'

'Lor', child! *I* don't know! 'Twas a lawyer's document of sorts – and no one must read *them* save the mistress or the master's clerk. And then only when the master asks!'

'Then how do you know it was a lawyer's document?' Smith said this with desperate sharpness, for he was coming back to life with a vengeance.

Meg, seeing nothing but the boy's improvement and wanting to humour him, smiled confidentially. ''Twas marked for the attorneys, Billing and Lennard . . . with 'oom we 'ave dealings.' She sighed sentimentally. 'Billing and Cooing I call 'em – on account of Mr Billing being sweet on Miss Mansfield. He's in the parlour now. Such a handsome pair!' Her smile grew soft and misty – then she remembered Smith's question. 'So what else *could* it have been but one of the master's documents? Answer me that!'

Dazedly, Smith nodded. What else could it have been but one of the magistrate's documents?

For what would a light-fingered alley-scuttler like Smith be doing with a document marked for a lawyer?

'Did – did you give it to 'im?'

'To our Mr Billing? Lor', no! That's for the master to do! Besides, it were for the other one, for Mr Lennard.'

'So you g-gave it to Mister Mansfield?'

'Questions, questions! Was you a cat, you'd be stone dead! No: I never gave it to him. There. Why, it smelled so bad it would 'ave knocked him flat – what with 'is disability an' all! I put it in his study along with 'is other papers. Only I put it at the bottom so's the smell might wear off afore he comes to it! That's what makes a good servant,' she added proudly. 'Consideration for 'er master's feelings. Oho! There's a good lad! Drunk up your ale! Just 'omesick, weren't you? Knew it all the time. Trust Meg!'

She repeated this several times with some triumph, then beamed encouragingly at Smith and left the room. On the way downstairs she sniffed and tossed her head in high contempt and muttered: 'Chills and fevers and sulphury poisonings? 'Omesick! Ha! And it took a motherly soul like Meg to see it. Brains? Give you a farthing for 'em!'

She prodded the snoozing footman and boasted of Smith's improvement.

'A touch of 'eart,' she said. 'That's all this big busy Town 'as need of! Take that boy, f'rinstance . . .'

It was now midnight and, to Miss Mansfield's aggravation and distress, Mr Billing stayed for another hour. Then at last he went, and, when her father was safely in bed, she flew upstairs with an anguished heart – expecting she knew not what.

She opened the door; she looked inside, and she all but dropped her candle. The room was empty! The boy was gone! Her face grew pale with dread. A terrible fear assailed her. The boy, feeling himself to be dying, had struggled from his bed and crept from the house. The housekeeper's grim words echoed in her mind. 'These little souls of the Town perish easily . . .'

In blackest despair she began to go downstairs. Suddenly, she stopped. She'd heard a noise: very gentle, very subtle, very secretive. A papery rustle. From her father's study.

She approached the door. She was much frightened and would have aroused the house – but an odd instinct prevented her. She opened the door. She held up the candle –

'Smith!'

'Oh my Gawd! I'm done for!'

The floor about Mr Mansfield's desk looked as though it had been snowed on by documents! Depositions, Confessions, Summonses and Judgments lay in a guilty profusion, and in the midst of them crouched Smith, wearing only his shirt and looking like an outsize document himself with his face turned up like a grey seal of terror!

All Miss Mansfield's dread and anguish turned now into a violent fury and bitterness.

'*Smith!* Is this how you repay Mr Mansfield? By robbing him? Stealing from a blind man? Is *this* the kindness of heart that so moved him? Nothing but the cunning skill of a cruel rogue?'

She spoke in a trembling whisper – for she dared not awake her father.

Smith, still among the documents, stared up at her with a mixture of misery and fear. He'd not yet found his precious document, which he knew he'd have recognized even among the hundreds he'd strewn about. Now he was done for. Flight was impossible. Miss Mansfield stood in the doorway, and the builder had provided no other way out. He wondered what would be done with him. The worst he could count on was being taken and hanged for a thief. The best – to be sent furiously out into the night. Either way, the document was lost for ever.

'I – I ain't cruel,' he mumbled unhappily. 'Reely, I ain't . . .'

Miss Mansfield bit on her lip. She scowled – and her face in the candlelight looked like a small thundercloud. Fiercely, she continued to stare at the unlucky Smith. Really! What could one expect of such a child? All his life a thief! She began to grow angry with her father again. He ought to have expected something like this. But he was so foolishly sentimental! Just because the boy showed him a kindness when any other wretch would have robbed him and left him for dead . . . why should he think Smith was exceptional? And reformed? A stupid idea. As if such a boy would change in an evening! It takes time. And her father, of all people, should have known!

Miss Mansfield's breast began to heave with aggravation, and Smith watched her piteously.

Her father was outrageous! Always he expected her to have the patience of a saint. Well – she hadn't! She was peevish. And now he'd left her to deal with the wretched boy while he slept on in happy ignorance. Oh!

'Smith,' she said at length, scowling worse than ever under the strain of her long inner quarrel. 'I – I'm disappointed, it's true. But – you're fortunate that Mr Mansfield is more understanding than his daughter. *She*, I promise you, would have had you clapped straight into Newgate! But Mr Mansfield never expected an angel out of you all at once. Mr Mansfield's a saint, Smith, and on that account you may thank your stars! Go back to bed this instant – and we'll say no more of tonight. But – if I catch you doing any such thing again – then it's Newgate for you, my lad, on the instant. Now – to bed! Don't gape. Don't cry! Tears won't move me. Or don't you understand, Smith? You've been given another chance.'

Chapter 8

The house in Vine Street was both joined to and separated from its neighbour by a brick-built arch that led to the stable and yard. This arch was so clumsy in its brickwork that, skilful as was the coachman, he was forever scraping the paintwork of Miss Mansfield's curricle and her father's coach. But nothing was ever done to remedy this; Mr Mansfield had grown used to the sound of it and Miss Mansfield would allow no change to anything that helped her father to see with his ears or hands.

So the carriages continued to be scraped and the stableboy was forever being sent to the paint shop for pigment or varnish to make good the damage. Which task fell naturally to Smith. It was on one of these journeys that he fell in with a certain muffin-man with whom he had an old street acquaintance.

'Ain't I seed you before?' asked the muffin-man, thrown out by Smith's cleanliness and livery.

'Maybe,' said Smith cautiously, and then decided to make use of the acquaintance.

'D'you know the Red Lion Tavern in Saffron Hill?'

The muffin-man grinned. He knew it all right.

'And d'you know the two ladies what reside in its nether regions?' (Smith's education had begun and he'd acquired a fanciful taste in words.)

'The darlings in the cellar? Miss Bridget and Miss Fanny? Everyone knows them!'

'The very same! I'd be obleeged if you'd carry 'em a message.'

The muffin-man thrust out his lower lip till it looked like the last quarter of a muffin.

'Tell 'em a – a *certain person's* well and prospering. Tell 'em 'e's on 'is way up in the world . . . and will communicate further when a suitable occasion has arose.'

Much impressed, the muffin-man nodded. 'I'll tell 'em.'

'Don't forget now. A certain person's on his way up in the world.'

Then, watched all the way by the admiring muffin-man, Smith strolled back to the house in Vine Street, whistling cheerfully – for he'd just discharged a duty that had been weighing on him these three weeks past; he'd set his sisters' minds at rest (always supposing they'd ever been otherwise), and so had kept his word with Mr Mansfield. He smiled somewhat wistfully as he pictured Miss Bridget's and Miss Fanny's face when they got his news. And he sighed when he thought of his friend, Lord Tom. Well – well . . . they weren't gone for ever. Some day, soon, they'd all meet again, when he'd got what he wanted from the document . . .

His face darkened. The document was still in Mr Mansfield's study and not all of his wit and deftness had brought him any nearer to recovering it. When he was in the house Miss Mansfield watched him like a brisk and suspicious hawk; and when he was in the yard the coachman watched him even sharper . . . while the three ugly, lumbering horses, Smith felt, kept more than an ordinary eye on him.

At night, he dared not try again, for Miss

Mansfield slept light as a feather . . . and she'd give him no second chance. His credit on her kindness was stretched to its limit and he shivered as he thought of its breaking. For he'd come, little by little, to think as well of the Mansfields as anyone else (Lord Tom and his sisters excepted) in the world.

Though both of them, on occasion, frightened him half to death, there were times when they did no such thing. There were times, even, when they made him grin: viz, when they quarrelled over which of them was to be blamed for a kindness. There were times when they made him shrug his shoulders in bewilderment: viz, when Miss Mansfield lit candles for her blind father and did everything to persuade the house he could see it . . . and yet she'd have nothing moved – be it ever so awkward and ill-placed – lest her father stumble against it and so betray what the whole world knew: viz, that he was blind as a mole. There were times when nothing pleased Smith more than Miss Mansfield's praise of his progress in reading, so that, for the moment, her good opinion seemed the chief purpose in his studying and not the document at all! Of which studying Meg the scullery maid took a vexatious view.

'Learning?' she'd say contemptuously, while

Smith sat in the kitchen of a late afternoon or evening, his small white face cupped in his thin white hands, staring up at Meg's big red face pillowed in her big red arms. 'Learning? Give you a farthing for it! Mark my words, little one – a yewmanbeen's better off without it! What good's it ever done a soul? Brains? Wouldn't have 'em if you paid me! A penn'orth of heart's worth all your skinny clever heads!' She stared thoughtfully at Smith's own skinny face and pushed over a piece of pie as if to fill him out as quickly as possible. 'I saw some clever heads – once. When I was a little girl. Me mother – God rest her – showed me. Three of 'em: a Lord, a Sir and a Mister. On the Traitors' Gate. Cut off at the neck! Very clever heads, they was. And much good it did 'em! "Meg!" said she – I'll always remember her words – "Meg! Take note. Heads without hearts is naught but bleeding pompoms! Of no use to man, woman or child."'

'But at least you can read, Meg,' said Smith, munching at the pie. 'For you read the name on that old paper you found when I was washed.'

Meg stared at him crossly, as if she felt all her warning were wasted. 'I can read what's proper and needful, young man! But no more than that. F'rinstance, I'd never read a *book*!'

'But what about Miss Mansfield?'

Meg shut her eyes in vexation.

'Yes! You look at the mistress. All trouble and worry and storms in the heart! And then you look at the master who can neither read nor write on account of his disability – which is, maybe, a blessing in disguise. All smiles and even-faced. All contentment, *I'd* say. There, now!' Surprised by her own powers of observation, she opened her eyes triumphantly. 'So who's the better off? Brains? Give you a farthing for 'em!'

But in spite of Meg's warnings Smith continued to study as hard as he was able. He mastered the alphabet – that sinister collection of twists and curls and crosses and gibbet-shaped signs that resembled nothing so much as the irons that hung on Newgate's most dreadful walls and, by the time of his meeting with the muffin-man, he could pronounce aloud such words as Miss Mansfield wrote on his slate.

'M-y n-a-m-e i-s S-m-i-t-h . . . th,' he sputtered out with great difficulty, only understanding the sentiment as he heard the sounds he made.

'Well done!' cried Miss Mansfield and Smith, though pleased to have pleased her, was mildly aggrieved to discover that so much effort had gone into saying aloud what was perfectly well known to both of them all the time. None the less, he was much encouraged and Miss Mansfield promised him that, in but a short while more, he'd be able to read whatever his heart desired. On which Smith's eyes would stray towards Mr Mansfield's study with an expression of great yearning and hope.

Sometimes, Mr Mansfield himself would stay to listen to Smith's lesson, now and then explaining something of which his poor blind eyes still held the memory. But mostly he kept silent, save when he, too, had occasion to praise the boy's quickness and progress. And this, when it happened, moved Smith oddly, for he sensed a deep generosity behind it, and if anything could bring tears to Smith's eyes (apart from a thump on the nose), it was the sudden warmth of a generous heart.

Nor were the Mansfields the only ones who were pleased by Smith's redemption from black ignorance – which was following so pat on his redemption from his other blackness. Mr Billing had come to hear of Miss Mansfield's pupil, and the lad's arrival and subsequent improvement at Miss Mansfield's hands formed a fresh subject for his lively chatter.

This Mr Billing was a handsome fellow of thirty

or thereabouts. He had rosy cheeks, a prosperous, dark moustache and eyes that, when they weren't shining with devotion to Miss Mansfield, were shining with all of an attorney's shrewdness and wit. He walked with quick springy steps and put off his cloak with an air. These facts Smith had learned from observing him from the dark top of the stairs, for, as Miss Mansfield had never yet seen fit to introduce the stable-boy to her suitor, Mr Billing and Smith had not yet met; even though he called often and unexpectedly, knowing that, in courtship, the sudden is worth its weight in gold.

Sometimes he'd come mid-morning with a, 'I was passing and couldn't resist', and sometimes mid-afternoon with a, 'I found myself at your door as if by magic!' Then there'd be much cheerful laughter and in he'd come and settle for an hour, dispensing pleasure to Miss Mansfield and irritation to Smith who would be banished to the kitchen. For Miss Mansfield preferred to break off the lesson rather than have her suitor and the stable-boy – whose tongue she couldn't answer for – meet face to face.

This uneasiness of hers persisted and even grew, and what at first had been a fleeting and foolish embarrassment became a deep and odd fear, so that a meeting she'd begun preventing almost lightly, became an affair of strange importance that must be avoided at all costs.

She'd grown deeply fond of Smith, who'd darted into her heart as neatly as she supposed he'd once darted from doorway to doorway in the freezing, friendless streets. An extraordinary child: a fascinating, quick-witted, dear-faced, obliging and determined child . . . but a child whose sometimes violent tongue she couldn't answer for, and whose resentment at Mr Billing's interruptions alarmed her. More and more, she came to dread the meeting she'd so far put off, but which she knew she could not put off for ever.

There's no doubt that, by keeping all this to herself, she'd helped it grow to formidable dimension in her mind; but Smith's resentment seemed to be growing likewise – as if his patience was running out. As if there was some goal he'd set his heart on, and the nearer he came to it the more enraged he was at being delayed.

Which was nothing less than the truth; for Smith was now very close to being able to read. His long battle was nearly won. Letters were making words for him; words were making sentences. Great pages of print that, scarce four weeks ago had seemed no more than a mad patterning of the paper, now spoke haltingly to him – even told stories – as if long-dead gentlemen woke up under his struggling eyes, button-holed his mind and breathed their thoughts and dreams into it. Gentlemen who were dead and dust a thousand years stirred and shifted and began to live their lives again.

But still there were gaps and lapses and conjunctions of letters that seemed to have no business together. He thought often of the document but he knew it was useless to him till he could fill those gaps and lapses. So he waited for the day when Miss Mansfield should declare, 'Smith: now you can read whatever your heart desires.'

But with the over-attentive attorney's interruptions that day did not come till a certain Tuesday morning when the event Miss Mansfield had tried so hard to prevent also came to pass, as sooner or later it had to.

'Well, Smith,' she said with a proud and affectionate smile, 'now all the wisdom of the world is yours for the taking. For you can read, my dear –'

On which Smith's heart leaped almost to the skies; and when there came at almost the self-same moment the familiar double knock on the front door, he felt, in place of his customary resentment, a grand relief that he could escape and caper and dance in private triumph.

'It's Mister Billing, miss!' he said with a cheerfulness that amazed Miss Mansfield. 'Come a-cooing! So I'll be off and 'ide meself now. The best of luck to you, miss! I'm sure you'll be very 'appy!'

With that, he fled from the library in high delight, and with the best will in the world (for Smith, when he wished anyone happiness, really meant it – happiness being a word he didn't use lightly), stopped in the hall to wish Mr Billing the same.

'Best of 'appiness in your cooing, Mister Billing!' he cried – then faltered on his way down the stairs.

The rosy-cheeked attorney had gone a deathly white. A look of wild amazement had come upon his face. His eyes had widened; his mouth had dropped open. A shudder had gone through him. Then, as abruptly as his colour had gone, so did he – without so much as a word for the lady of his heart. The door slammed violently and Smith, sensing he was the cause, went hastily to the kitchen, puzzled and vaguely alarmed.

About half an hour after he'd left, Mr Billing returned – and in a state of such high excitement, said the footman who'd admitted him, that he felt sure the gentleman had at last plucked up his courage to ask for the mistress's hand. He'd been shown into the library where the mistress and master were wondering on his unaccountable departure. The footman had listened long enough to hear Mr Billing declare that Miss Mansfield was looking handsomer than ever he could remember.

'So she is,' nodded Meg wisely. 'For love paints our faces something beautiful.'

Here, the housekeeper – a single lady with a complexion midway between a lemon and a turnip – muttered, 'Stuff and nonsense!' but looked very wistful; and Smith, whose uneasiness had taken a sharp turn for the worse on the attorney's return, said, 'Thank Gawd!'

The housekeeper looked at him curiously, and Smith, feeling the vague danger past, said, 'It was only that I thought 'e'd been took ill before,' and went on to relate the brief meeting which he'd previously kept to himself.

The coachman, who'd come into the kitchen for his morning mug of ale, shook his head with all the pessimism of a man whose days are spent reasoning with horses.

'Mark my words – he's most likely got a wife and

child in Clapham or somewheres an' the sight of our young Smith reminded him. Small wonder he went white. Any man would.'

'Stuff and nonsense!' declared the housekeeper looking even more wistful. 'Nothing but biliousness. There's a deal of it about. Just popped out to clear his head. Very sensible.'

But Meg was of the opinion that Mr Billing's sudden pallor and departure were due to nothing other than a brief loss of courage in his heart's intentions which he'd forthwith gone out to strengthen at the nearest tavern.

'I'll wager he'd a smell of brandy about him!' she said.

These three opinions now provoked the Vine Street household into a lively dispute for some minutes, during which the coachman's was rejected with contempt, and the housekeeper's thought the most likely – though it was Meg's that won the day. For the Vine Street household was of a sentimental and hopeful turn of mind and always looked forward to the time when Miss Mansfield's tempestuous person should be removed, happily, to another establishment.

The footman who'd answered the door now agreed that there *had* been a brandy-ish air about the attorney, and a parlourmaid who'd been listening at the library door came down with the news that the attorney seemed tongue-tied – a sure sign, for someone in his calling, of being in the last extreme of love.

On this, there was a general burst of smiling and pleasure and the unfortunate coachman had his elbow jogged as he sought to hide his pessimistic face in his mug of ale. Then Meg, in a mood of powerful tenderness, laid her large arm about Smith's shoulders and declared:

'And this little mite's the one who's brought it all on. The mistress has grown that tender since he's been with us. He's warmed her heart and opened it up to Mr Billing's cooing. It would never have come about without our little Smith. So give honour and kindness where the same are due!'

With that, she imprinted a large, moist kiss on Smith's surprised face. He blushed – and everyone laughed . . . including the coachman who laughed loudest of all. So in a matter of moments, Smith was become quite a hero, and when the parlour maid (who'd gone back to her post at the library door), came down with the news that Smith was wanted, everyone – even Smith himself – was convinced it was because Miss Mansfield wanted to show off the wonders she'd worked in him. He got off his chair and straightened his coat. The housekeeper found a comb and brought order to his hair. A footman wiped a smut off his face; another suggested a quick bath – and chuckled.

'Go on up, Smith!' – 'Do us all proud, Smith!' – 'God bless you, Smith!' – 'Don't forget, Smith – we're all behind you, lad!'

And so they were, for, as Smith went proudly up the stairs, the Vine Street household followed closely after to give him a last pat on the back as he knocked on the library door and went inside.

It was just on midday. A brisk fire was burning in the library, for the weather was turned very bitter and the sky bulged with unshed snow. For a second time Smith and Mr Billing stared at one another; and for a second time the attorney shuddered – to the depths of his soul, it seemed.

'It is him. This is the boy I saw. In the court. This boy stabbed Field. I saw him! He is the murderer! My poor friends – how monstrously you've been deceived!'

Mr Billing was the man from Godliman Street: the same man who'd questioned the unlucky bookseller.

Chapter 9

Great hopes, great joy, great trust, when they fail, do so swiftly – in a bleak and evil instant. They do not diminish little by little so that a man you trusted yesterday, today you trust a little less. He is lost, damned; nothing of him remains but is false as quicksand –

'Snake! Venomous little snake!'

From outside of the library door, where the Vine Street household was gathered, eager and close, to hear its prodigy's triumph, came this single, bitter, trembling voice.

'Snake!'

Whether it was the housekeeper's, a footman's, the coachman's – no one knew. It was of no consequence. It was the voice of the household, shaken and shocked out of its pleasant dream by the dreadful words of the attorney.

Within the library the brisk fire still danced and gleamed on the polished wood, the calm brown walls and the gilded backs of the books.

Miss Mansfield – elegant, handsome and gay in a yellow brocaded dress – had lost every scrap of her complexion. She'd put her hand to her face as if to hide from the world her horror and dismay. She cried: 'No! No! It's not so! You're mistook, sir! Not this boy! Never, I tell you!' But in her heart of hearts she could not but believe the attorney, not because she wanted to, but because she dreaded it was so.

'It is the boy I saw from my window in Curtis Court. I saw him struggle. I saw him stab. I saw him escape. There is no doubt. I wish to God there was. Forgive me . . .'

The attorney spoke low and shakingly, but his

eyes were cold as stone. If anything gleamed or flickered in them, the terrified Smith never saw it. If anything pricked in that subtle, black and dreadful place that he suddenly divined was the attorney's heart, there was nothing to show for it. Save once. When Miss Mansfield cried out for a second time, there was in her voice such a world of misery that Mr Billing's white hands clenched and he seemed to flinch – as if his real love for Miss Mansfield had moaned: You're murdering me, Thomas Billing!

Miss Mansfield moved – and the rustling of her dress was as a dragging sigh. She crossed the room to her father – that motionless man in his high-backed chair. She made to lay her hand on his (which was fixed upon his stick), but he sensed her intention and waved her off. The customary blandness of his face seemed carved out of granite.

While Smith – Smith, who'd done nothing – *could* do nothing but moan in a dreadful amazement several times over, 'You're mad! You're mad! I never laid a finger on the old man! I never touched the old man! I never – never – never . . .' He retreated from them and began to glare very hopelessly about the room . . . to Miss Mansfield, to the window (against which stood the sorrowful, terrible attorney), to the door behind which was the Vine Street household.

No way out. Thoughts – such as they were – whirled in his head and made him feel sick. The blow that had fallen was inexplicable, frightful, crushing. He crept to Mr Billing. Stared up at him very piteously.

'You – you was wrong, Mister Billing! For Gawd's sake, tell 'em! For you're a-killing me!'

But the attorney shook his handsome head.

'Not wrong, Smith. I saw. I know.'

'Then damn you!' shouted Smith and flew to the Mansfields – blind father and tragic daughter.

'Miss! You knows me! I never done it! Swear on the Scriptures! Swear! Swear! You believe me, Miss Mansfield? *Please* –'

In an inward agony Miss Mansfield stared down at Smith . . . and then to the sad but certain attorney – who seemed to have no reason in the world to lie. Maybe she remembered the Smith who'd first come to her – and tried to rob her blind father's study? Maybe she thought the boy's fall was a punishment for her own pride in imagining she'd redeemed him? Who can tell what went on in her unhappy soul!

'Oh, Smith!' she whispered, and turned away.

'Then damn you, too! You Bedlam-mad saint!' wept Smith helplessly, and bent down, crouching, at the magistrate's feet: his old blind justice . . . his mole-in-the-hole.

'Mister Mansfield! You believe me. I know it. I can see it in your – your . . . You know me – and I know you. You know I never done him in!'

But the magistrate – to whom justice was the only fixed thing in a dark, uncertain world – said nothing. He was casting out of his heart and mind everything save the attorney's measured words and the urchin's frantic denials. Word against word.

'Mister Mansfield!' whispered Smith, staring up and seeing his own face distortedly reflected in the blind man's black spectacles. 'You *must* believe! It wasn't me! It was them two men in brown and –'

'– Two men in brown?'

'Yes! Yes! And –'

'– You saw them kill him?'

'I – I –'

'Yet you told me once you'd never seen Mr Field!'

Too late! Smith realized he'd ruined himself! Now he was done for.

The blind man sighed like the winter wind.

'So . . . so . . . it was you who killed him.'

The world fell away, and Smith, still crouching on the floor and watching the blind man's lips, felt as lonely, bitter and forlorn as if he were already on the gallows. Softly, the blind man went on:

'Which hand did you use, Smith? Was it the one you gave me that night we met? Was it that same, small, helping hand? Tell me, Smith! Don't be ashamed – for didn't I say to you that devils and angels are all one to me?'

'Voices in the night!' muttered Smith, despairingly. 'We're all voices in the night to you – you poor old blind fool!'

'You will be committed to prison to await your trial.'

'Trial? What d'you want to try me for? Might as well do me in now. What's one voice less in your noisy night, Mister Magistrate Mansfield? You'll never see me face when I'm nubbed. Nothing'll haunt you! You done right, you have! All I 'ope is – fer your sake and mine – that if you goes to heaven, then I goes to hell! For I wouldn't want you to clap even dead eyes on me!'

'Smith –'

'I never done it, Mister Mansfield.'

'You'll be tried –'

'– And nubbed!'

'God have mercy on your soul!'

'Not if He's a blind old gent like you!'

'Smith –'

But Smith did not say another word. He shook his head with an air of grimness and despair. He had retired a great way within himself and whatever he found there seemed to absorb him entirely.

He was much mishandled as he was bundled into the coach, for the Vine Street household were very bitter and outraged by the monstrousness of Smith. Even those who, but an hour before, had decided once and for all that there was much goodness in him and had vowed never again to judge by appearances – even they thrust bleak and savage faces close to his, to let him know what the world now thought.

There was a good deal of treading on his feet and jerking of his clothes. Two of his bright buttons were torn off and the side of his face was bruised. But all he did was to shake his head endlessly . . . even to the one kindly face that managed to push its way in among all the anger and contempt to look at him through the coach window. It was Meg, the scullery maid. Her eyes were as large and round and wet as Margate oysters.

'I'll come and see you, dear. I'll bring you something nourishing. Don't fret, little Smith. Meg won't forget you, dear!'

In the general commotion something had been forgotten, or would have been but for the scrupulous attorney.

'Wait! Wait!' he shouted from the window. 'The warrant!'

The warrant was sworn and witnessed.

'I'll take it down, sir.'

The magistrate nodded, wearily.

'And I'll go with him to the gaol.'

'There's no need, Billing. There's no need for you to endure any more.'

'I'll go, sir. It – it's the least I can do. Let the wretched child have some company on his journey. I'll see him decently lodged.'

Miss Mansfield raised her eyes to Mr Billing. Their look much moved him.

'We thank you, sir, for this – kindness.' She sighed. 'I blame myself for this. It was I who encouraged the boy. My father was not a party to it. But he was too kind to urge his better judgement. And now – and now –' She spread out her hands and shook her head. Then she seemed to recover herself somewhat and frowned in a semblance of her old manner. 'Papa! You have a donkey for a daughter! A sentimental foolish donkey! So we must be thankful for Mr Billing who's proved himself the best and truest of friends!' She curtsied. 'Your servant, sir. Your very humble servant!'

The coach was waiting, much scraped from a more than ordinary collision with the uneven arch. Within crouched Smith, wiping from his face what the coachman had spat in it.

'To Newgate!' ordered the attorney, and joined his victim.

The coach moved off and, for a little way, the two occupants stared at each other: the one, incredulously – the other, calmly. Then, when the wheels had settled down to a steady, loud rattle, Mr Billing leaned forward.

The skin round his eyes puckered somewhat – as if to suggest a smile. But his eyes were still like stone.

'Give it to me, boy.'

Dully, Smith began to comprehend. He stared back at the attorney with violent hatred.

'For God's sake, boy! There's not much time!

Give it to me – the paper you stole from the old man. Let me have it – and you can go.'

'I ain't got it.'

'And I know you have!'

'Search me – or are you afraid of being bit? For I'm a venomous little snake, I am!'

The attorney looked at the boy sharply; then withdrew the hand he'd held out. He shook his head with a curious air of gentleness.

'All right, lad – I believe you. What was in it?'

'Don't know.'

'Then – where is it?'

'Don't know.'

'Don't your life mean a fig to you?'

'Don't know.'

Mr Billing compressed his lips, then shook his head again with the same strange gentleness as before. He sighed.

'You're foolish, young man. I promise I'll help you, but you must tell me. It's your only chance. All right – all right! Keep silent now, if you must. I'll understand. But believe me, young Smith, I'm your truest friend! And soon you'll come to see it. Not today, nor even tonight – but tomorrow, maybe. I'll visit you, boy – and we'll talk again. Lay our cards on the table, eh? And then – and then, who knows, but we may be friends? You and me, Smith. Don't look so despairing, son. I'm not a villain. It's this vile world we live in, boy!'

But Smith continued to look despairing; the blow that had befallen him was more terrible, even, than the attorney guessed at. The document was lost and, though at last he could have read it, it was further away from him now than ever it had been since he'd picked Mr Field's pocket. It had brought him nothing but disaster, but it seemed his life depended on it. He hated it; he dreaded it; yet it was as though he'd sold his soul for it.

'Newgate Gaol, sir!' shouted the coachman, grimly.

Mr Billing sighed – and Smith groaned . . . while the birds on Old Bailey and St Paul's screeched out in high triumph:

'Jug him! Jug – jug – jug him!'

At last, they were about to be obliged.

Chapter 10

There lay in Newgate a very famous felon whose days were drawing to a close. Indeed, on this Wednesday, there was less than a fortnight's life left in him; on Tuesday, January twenty-third, Dick Mulrone was to be taken out and hanged. A great many petitions had been got up to save him, but none had succeeded, and no one in his heart of hearts was truly sorry, for the death of a hero (even though he was a murderous ruffian) was a vastly romantic thing.

From morning to night there was a press of carriages outside the gaol – for Mr Mulrone had more friends and admirers than he knew what to do with. They came to see him, to talk with him, even to drink with him, and then go away and brood on the frailty of human life (Mr Mulrone's, not their own).

Even great ladies came and went – their huge skirts swinging and pealing down the doleful passages like so many brocaded bells, tolling:

What a pity. What a shame. Dick's to die on Tuesday week. What a pity. What a shame. Poor Mr Mulrone.

So it was that Smith, and his bitterness and bewilderment with all the world, dropped into Newgate with no more stir than a driblet of spittle into the Fleet Ditch. True, the gaoler at the lodge had been surprised when he'd discovered that the undersized object in livery was Smith.

'Not old Smith?' he'd said, with a shrug and a grin. 'Not grubby little Smith? Thieving Smith, Smith o' the doorways and corners? Smith o' the stinking Red Lion?'

Then he'd thrust his reeking, bristly face close and remarked on Smith's cleanliness and said he'd never suspected his features were so human.

'But washing ain't exackly been profitable, eh?

For yore dirt, Smith, hid a multitude o' sins and now them sins is exposed to the view, so here you are, me lad! Gaoled, jugged and bottled – as we say in the trade!'

But when he learned the charge was murder, he withdrew somewhat and said reproachfully: 'Ah now, Smith – that's bad! Poor Miss Fanny and Miss Bridget. When they comes to alter them clothes – why, they'll wash 'em with their tears!'

Smith was lodged in the Stone Hall, but was spared fetters on account of Mr Billing's having paid the gaoler the necessary dues; which charitable act had been accompanied by a whispered, 'Don't take it too hard, lad!' and a look as deep as the ocean. Then the Stone Hall was locked and Smith was, for the first time, a resident in it and not a visitor. Which was a dark and lonely time for him . . .

Though he'd been shut in the Stone Hall as a kindness – there being worse places in the gaol where he might fairly have been lodged – he dreaded meeting with old acquaintances now his circumstances were so come down. He shrank from Mr Palmer and his friends, for he remembered, burningly, that he'd last departed from them with some defiance, being on his way up in the world.

Mercifully, he was spared Mr Palmer's sneers and scorn. The gentleman was otherwise engaged. Indeed, all the superior debtors were, at that time, too full of Dick Mulrone's grand visitors to spare a glance for the dismal, fearful, pallid child who crept from corner to corner like a persecuted ghost.

The only soul to pay him any heed had been an old man who'd not seen daylight for fifteen years. This queer old fettered bird slept in the fireplace all the year round, save on Christmas Day when the fire was lit (when with much good-natured laughter they shovelled him out), and had come to resemble a dusty ember.

He beckoned Smith over with four or five sharp gestures and offered to share his strange nest. Salubrious, he said it was, owing to a good down draught from the chimney. With a clank of his fetters, he pointed upward to the ragged black hole and declared that sometimes a star might be seen, twinkling away like it was sat on Newgate's roof.

'It ain't so bad, little sparrow. You gets used to it. Though we never sees the sun, we never gets doused by the rain, neither! And it's a comfort to know you're in the worst place in the world . . . so you've naught more to fret and slave about to keep yourself from falling lower. For you've arrived!'

Then he settled back on his haunches and appeared to doze off, leaving Smith to stare up into the darkness. From time to time the old man – now sunk into a nesting coil – would twitch and jerk in a curious fashion, bringing his chained wrists together and thumping them down as if on a hated head. This done, he'd sigh and settle down once more into a contented sleep . . . till the next time.

Smith shivered and wondered if the old man, too, had his Billing and Mansfields to plague his very sleep. Smith had come to hate the Mansfields more, even, than he hated Mr Billing. Once he'd admired and even loved them. He'd respected them and trusted them. He had, so to speak, made great exports from his heart towards them and had reasonably expected some sort of return. But at the first squall, they'd defaulted – bankrupted Smith – and left him in a state of blind rebellion. If ever Mr Billing was able to get him out of the gaol, Smith would make it his business to take a good revenge on the saints of Vine Street.

This resolution, in part, calmed him, though the mystery that clung about Mr Billing, the document and – worst of all – about the unseen man with the limp, remained as dark and menacing as ever.

Next day, at about ten o'clock in the morning,

Smith had visitors: Miss Bridget and Miss Fanny. He was both pleased and surprised. How had they learned so soon! Miss Bridget sighed bitterly, and remarked that bad news travels quick; while it took three weeks to learn that Smith was going up in the world, it took but the same number of hours to discover he was come down.

'And a common gaoler had to tell us! Oh! The shame of it! The degradation!'

Dismally, Smith picked at his brass buttons and neat coat.

'Fine clothes and a clean face are but the trappings of shame,' went on Miss Bridget, with furious sorrow, 'when the child what has them is so degradingly jugged. Oh!'

'I never done it!' said Smith. 'You know I never done it.'

'You're here, ain't you?' said Miss Bridget unhappily. 'That speaks volumes, don't it? You done something!'

'I was wrongly accused! Victimized!'

Said Miss Fanny: 'Innocence is no excuse in the eyes of the Law, Smut dear. *That* much your sisters know!'

They stared at him angrily and tragically, while he looked back with as much of defiance as he could manage; then Miss Fanny, as was her nature, thought of a brighter side. She sighed and poked at her remarkable hat (for whenever the sisters came out of their cellar, they dressed very grandly indeed – as an advertisement of their taste and skill).

'Leastways, 'tis lucky you picked on such a time to get nabbed, sweet. For with dear Dick Mulrone in residence the tone goes up, don't it! My, but there's fashion and elegance coming and going. Don't you think, Brid, 'twill do our Smut good to be mixing with such gentility? As I always said, 'tis an ill wind that don't blow the silver lining out of the dreariest cloud!'

She sipped genteelly at her gin – they were in the taproom – and made a face. Miss Bridget, who was drinking ale, put down her pot and looked at her sister scornfully.

'Much good his gentility will do him when that disgusting Mr Jones has done with him! It's his clothes that'll be coming down our steps with no boy inside of them, Fanny. And have you thought, sister, what it'll cost to have possession of him for to bury him proper and decent? Or would you have him be took off to Surgeons' Hall to be bottled for all the world to jeer at?'

Miss Fanny shivered and shook her head; then

she murmured: 'Oh, Smut, dear – if only you'd given up the dockiment when Lord Tom asked, then there'd be no Surgeons' Hall, nor Mr Jones – nor even them two fierce gents in brown –'

'Did they come back, then?' muttered Smith, coming out of his pint pot of ale, where he'd been hiding his face while his sisters disposed of his remains.

Yes, they'd come back . . . and back again. They'd haunted the Red Lion for several days. A terrible pair with eyes like burning coals . . . though the taller of them (said Miss Fanny) might have been more presentable if he'd been on the snaffling lay instead of on the sneaking, throat-slitting budge . . .

Here, Miss Bridget remarked that Miss Fanny's language was as bad as her low-class friend's. To which Miss Fanny said gently that she liked to find good in everyone and that, had it not been for dear Lord Tom, the villains in brown might still have been there.

'He took them on one side, Smut, and spoke to them so fierce, that they've never been back since that moment!'

Then Miss Fanny went off into a melancholy memory of how cheered they'd been to get the good news. Which had the effect of disheartening Smith into miserable tears.

Round about them the dregs of the Town ebbed and shuffled and flowed in ever-changing groups and pairs, sometimes eyeing Smith and his visitors with sneering curiosity, but more often discussing the latest news of doomed Mulrone.

Smith's fireplace companion alone seemed to keep his interest; he crouched but two yards off, with his head on one side and his old, bleared eyes quite sharp – like an ancient parrot. Contrary to her usual habit, Miss Fanny saw no good in him at all, but shuddered to the depths of her soul whenever his old, old eyes caught hers.

At length, to Smith's great pleasure and pride, Lord Tom joined them. He'd come from paying his respects to his old comrade-in-arms, Dick Mulrone. He wore a melancholy, romantic air like a new green cloak and seemed to swirl it from the tips of his ragged eyelashes to the ends of his powder-stained fingers.

'Well, Smut, me lad! Alas, it seems you've forestalled me! Not lost, but gone before, eh?' He sighed, 'Oh, me boy! You go in good company: the best i' the world. For, though I'm a Finchley Common man and poor Dick's a Hounslow Heath boy, I give him best! The grandest of the roisterers! The gayest, dashingest, noblest of us all! He's in good spirits, lad. Ha-ha! The best! For he's drunk as a lord!'

'Disgusting!' muttered Miss Bridget and drew her discreet finery as close to her person as her hoops allowed. Lord Tom sat back with a toby-sized sigh and his glittering eyes roamed the stinking, shadowy, shuffling room with a touch of compassion – or was it only dread?

Smith looked very piteously from his sisters to his grand friend and the world seemed – even in the Stone Hall – too fair a place to be leaving after so few years in it. Suddenly, Lord Tom's eyes flickered – as if some distant shade had provoked a thought. He bent forward to his small friend.

'But we'll see, me fine lad! Yes, we'll see! While there's life, there's hope – as we say on the lay. Maybe Mr Jones won't have you yet awhile? Maybe Lord Tom can help?'

Smith, though not convinced, was sensible of Lord Tom's aim to be cheerful. He looked up with a mournful smile.

'How, Lord Tom?'

'That document, young fellow! D'you have it still?'

'N-not with me, Lord Tom.'

The highwayman looked doubtful – then brightened again.

'But d'you know where it lies?'

'That I do, Lord Tom!'

'And, given certain circumstances – such as you might know best – could you lay your hands on the afore-mentioned property?'

'That I could, Lord Tom!'

'And would you, me boy?'

'That I would, Lord Tom! With all me heart!'

'Then we'll see, me bright young heart. Dark though these matters be, while Lord Tom's about there's yet a ray of light.'

Lord Tom spread out his strong arms to escort Miss Fanny and Miss Bridget away. One arm was took but the other was left like an empty bracket: Miss Bridget had no need of support. She fidgeted with her hands and then, with a strange timidity, stretched out and fleetingly touched Smith's sunken head.

'Be back tomorrow, you – you felonious child! Just remember . . . though you be . . . not so good as you ought . . . you ain't forgot, dear. Fan and me'll be back!'

When Smith raised his head they were gone, but on the table beside his empty pot was a guinea.

Which one had left it? Smith scratched his head – and looked to the old man who seemed to have gone off into a dozy brood. The old man yawned and his eyes flickered.

'Ah! Me sparrow. That would be telling, wouldn't it? Which one cares a guinea's worth? The pigeon? The starling? Or that seedy hawk? He-he! It's worse than not knowing who's done you an injury – not knowing who's done you a kindness. It's horrible not knowing who to thank!'

But before Smith could abuse the old man, another visitor came quickly towards him. He and Smith's earlier visitors must have crossed paths without knowing it. It was Mr Billing.

He wore black, which gave his complexion an oddly high, artificial air. The old man looked at him uneasily and then clanked farther off – as if anticipating the attorney's wish. He turned his bony head and seemed to absorb himself in a corner.

'Well, lad,' murmurmed Mr Billing, sitting down and fingering the guinea idly. 'As you see, I've not forgot you.'

'No, Mister Billing,' muttered Smith, watching his money being scratched at by a neatly polished claw, 'I don't suppose you 'ave. And I've not forgot you, Mister lying Billing – Mister murdering Billing.

Not till Mister Jones turns me off up the road will I forget you! And if there's sich a thing as ghosts, Mister conniving Billing, there'll be a screaming, shrieking ghost awaiting you for every night of your life when you goes to bed!'

The attorney looked momentarily taken aback by the force of Smith's gloomy hate. Was it possible he hadn't expected it?

'I – I'm not a bad lot, y'know. I live in the world, so to speak . . . and can't help being of it. Take me all in all, I'm no worse than anyone else. Believe me, young man, you'll come to see that! Life's a race for rats . . . and it's Devil take the hindmost, the foremost – *and* the one in the middle. We're all rats, Smith – and it's eat or be eaten. Blame nature, if you like – but don't blame me!'

Having delivered himself of this, Mr Billing contrived to look oddly wistful – as if he wished the world were constituted otherwise and he might then be as honourable a man as could be met with in a month of Sundays.

Smith looked up at him dubiously – but couldn't help observing that, no matter what melancholy sincerity there was in the attorney's face, his fingers continued to play with the guinea like a cat with a fledgling bird.

'All right, then,' sighed Mr Billing at length, administering a final tap to the coin and blinking his stony eyes. 'Don't trust me. I don't blame you. No! If I was in your situation, I suppose I'd be just as suspicious. Good God! It's human nature! But I'll tell you here and now, my friend (and I *do* think of you as my friend, Smith . . . I like you, you know), I'll have you know I've saved your life!'

'By having me nubbed?' asked Smith, much bewildered by the talkative attorney. Mr Billing smiled playfully and shook his head.

'They knew you were in Vine Street, Smith.'

'Who did?'

'The two men in brown. And they'd have come to murder you if I'd done nothing and left you there.'

'Ain't they your friends, then, Mister Billing?'

The attorney looked about him quickly – then bent forward so's his red lips were close to Smith's dusty ear and his sharp moustache pricked and scraped almost painfully.

'Listen, friend,' he whispered. 'I'll lay my cards on the table. Open and above-board. I'll not lie to you – for I like you. We're two of a kind, Smith, you and me. Men who know what's what in the world. Eyes open, chins up – and outface the Devil!'

Despite himself, Smith felt flattered, for he was

but twelve and small, while Mr Billing was a grown man . . . He began to think less harshly of Mr Billing. A rogue he might be, but at least he was being an open one. He did indeed lay his cards on the table – and a very grubby pack they were! Though, as Mr Billing himself pointed out with a wry laugh, all cards get soiled when you play with 'em!

Yes, indeed, Mr Billing and the two men in brown had once been concerned with each other . . .

'Did they *'ave* to kill the old man?' muttered Smith dismally. 'Were it necessary?'

The attorney shrugged his shoulders.

'Ask Mr Black, my friend.'

Smith shivered, and once more his blood was uncannily chilled.

'W-was he the *other* one? The one I heard? The one with the limp?'

'More than a limp, Smith. A wooden leg. Very softspoken man. Very devilish. I don't think I'd like to meet with Mr Black on a dark night!'

The attorney paused and looked uneasily about him, as if he expected soft-spoken Mr Black to limp out of a shadow and knife him where he sat.

'Right, my lad! I'll lay my cards on the table . . .' (Here, Smith wondered, bemusedly, whether this was the same pack or a second one.)

'That document's worth money. A vast deal of money. Enough for you and me and the chimney-sweep down the road! I mean our friend, Mr Black. For I tell you, young man, I see no way of keeping him out of it. None! He's got the pair of us, Smith! We're the little running rats – and he's the gobbling Devil! If only, Smith – ah, if only –'

'If only what, Mister Billing?'

'You and me . . . just you and me . . . Where did you leave the document?'

'In –' began Smith; then something distracted him. The fettered old man. Was he having a fit? He was banging his chained wrists down on the floor.

'Where, Smith? Where?'

But Smith had suddenly thought more deeply.

'Lorst me memory, Mister Billing.'

'What d'you mean?'

'Strain of waiting to be nubbed, Mister Billing. Can't remember a thing. Leastways, not while I'm 'ere.'

'Don't you trust me, friend?'

Smith stared into the attorney's reproachful face and slowly shook his head.

'No, Mister Billing. I've had enough of trust to last the rest of me life.'

A dreadful bitterness had come back into Smith's

small pointed face, making it seem as old as the hills. Mr Billing's smooth cheeks seemed to pale somewhat. He murmured something about Smith 'sleeping on it' and that he'd see him tomorrow. Then he stood up and began to move away, trying to hold Smith's eyes till the shuffling ragbag of Newgate inhabitants got between him and his prey.

For long minutes Smith stared after him, not moving till he was taken up with the sounds of a commotion that seemed to be flowing through the prison's veins. A rumour: Dick Mulrone had been pardoned! But, even before that rumour had gone its rounds, its contradiction was already at its heels. No pardon. Poor Dick Mulrone's prospects were like a wave in the sea – forever followed by its trough. Twelve more days remained to him and Mr Jones, being Welsh and tuneful and fanciful, had already begun his Tyburn Carol:

> 'On the first day of counting
> My true love sent to me,
> A felon in an elm tree.'

'That's my boy!' wheezed the old man, recovered from his fit. 'Voice like a blooming nightingale!'

Chapter 11

They say the Devil is a bald man with spectacles, but Smith thought of him as being rosy-cheeked, with a prosperous moustache and a shrewd sense of a bargain when he saw one.

In his first nights in Newgate Smith dreamed many times of the Devil and what terms he might get for his soul. He had long conversations with him in which the Devil offered him escape, vengeance on the Mansfields, and enough money for himself, Mr Billing *and* the chimney-sweep down the road – and all for a little future frying.

'I like you, Smith,' the Devil murmured. 'We're both men of the world, and I'm partial to you. Particularly fried.'

Which prospect didn't seem as horrible as it might have done, for nights in the Stone Hall were that dismal and cold that the thought of any fire – even hell's – was agreeable. Also, these nights were unnaturally long and hard to sleep in. There were continual mutterings and mumblings and sudden cryings out. There was the clinking of leg-irons which sounded – when it was regular – like an endless chain being winched into some deep pit. While from far off – from that part of the gaol that was called The Castle, where wealthy felons and prisoners of State paid high money for their lodging – came the faint sounds of singing and good cheer as Dick Mulrone was swigged and swilled on his way to his end.

'On the fourth day of counting
My true love sent to me –
Four sextons digging,
Three parsons praying,
Two horses drawing,
And a felon in an elm tree.'

On which, Smith's ancient fireplace companion would moan and wheeze and finally wake up with a, 'That's my boy!' and jingle into a sitting position from which he'd watch Smith with deceiving bright eyes.

'Looking for the Newgate star?' he'd begin, for Smith usually lay with his eyes wide open and fixed on the ragged black hole above.

Then the old man would mumble and mutter about Smith's visitors and what they'd had to say. He missed nothing and it seemed, at times, as if pecking up scraps of other folks' business was the only thing that kept him alive.

Of all Smith's visitors he was most inquisitive about Mr Billing, whom he regarded as a 'real caution of a gent', and 'one to be handled with the tongs'.

Mr Billing had come to see Smith each day, sometimes only for minutes, but at other times for an hour or more. Once he met Miss Bridget and Miss Fanny and exchanged the briefest of courtesies with them, then left almost directly, saying he'd be out of place in family discussions. Miss Fanny was much impressed by him and even Miss Bridget had to admit he was 'quite gentlemanly to the look'. All of which gave Smith a certain gloomy pride – though he never admitted to more than 'legal business' between himself and the visiting attorney and so left his sisters most respectfully puzzled. But no matter whether Mr Billing stayed long or short, he contrived to strengthen his acquaintance with Smith by unexpected touches of humour and warmth.

He scarce ever referred to the document again for it was as plain as a pikestaff there'd be no escape without it. Once or twice he spoke of Mr Black, but it was only to say that, thank God, that evil man had not shown himself. Also, he begged Smith to be on his guard against such a visitor, though he doubted if Mr Black would dare to show his face in Newgate. He hinted also of 'a departure from this place to pastures new . . . which was being thought of, never fear! Was the other matter, likewise in hand?' To which Smith had nodded very gloomily indeed.

This sadness of his had been carefully observed by the ancient eavesdropper who taxed Smith with it that night.

'You ain't got it, have you!' he said triumphantly.

'Got what?'

'What he wants. So you'll have to stay!' He looked pleased as Punch at the thought of Smith being his companion for ever.

'You mind yer own business!' muttered Smith savagely, and glared the old man's beam off his face.

'Ain't got none to mind,' said the old man forlornly, and Smith relented somewhat and explained dismally: 'If I stays, they'll nub me!'

But the old man seemed not to have heard him for he stared vacantly into the air for several minutes, then slowly closed up his eyes and went to sleep still sitting, and leaving Smith to worry himself into a state of sick desperation.

His trial was already fixed: January twenty-third, the very day they were nubbing Dick Mulrone. 'Swing out the old, swing in the new', so to speak.

Smith came to thinking his fate and Mr Mulrone's were somehow linked and if the highwayman perished, then he'd not be long after. Eight more days had Dick Mulrone. How many had Smith?

The document! The cursed document! Furiously, he shut his eyes and tried to picture it, hoping his new skill in reading would reveal – from his mind's eye – what Mr Billing wanted to know. But, alas, he could make no more of it now than when he'd looked at it in his darkest ignorance. His mind's eye showed him nothing but a spidery jumble. Not having understood what he'd seen, he'd not known what to remember.

He wondered if Miss Mansfield had come upon the document yet – and if it had meant anything to her. He sweated with terror at the thought of her giving it to the attorney for nothing.

'Oh Gawd!' whispered Smith, staring up into the blackness of the chimney as if for an answer. 'Why did the old gent have to stuff his pockets with sich deadly papers? What right 'ad 'e to go stumping through the streets, 'eavy with the Devil's literature for to tempt the likes of me with?'

He shook his head and groaned and groaned at the misery of his lot – and wondered if he'd be hanged without ever discovering what he was being hanged for.

Smith's hopes were low. Only one held out any promise: Meg, the scullery maid from Vine Street. And then, at last, she came.

She'd kept her word even though a heavy fall of snow had begun during the night and was not yet done with. Her shawl and bonnet were grandly dappled with it and her nose had been whipped by the wind to a strawberry . . . but she'd brought Smith some veal pie, sausage and white bread. Also two shirts he'd left behind. She'd have come earlier – but she'd been that afraid of having her heart broke, she'd not dared leave the kitchen.

'You pore thing,' she said, giving him the bundle. 'Oh, you pore thing!' She gazed at him sadly. 'You've grown smaller and wizender. You needs feeding up, and – not meaning to be personal, dear – you needs another good wash!'

Smith shuddered at the memory and began to unwrap his bundle while Meg looked about her at the skinny, blotched and sadly cunning faces that haunted the Stone Hall.

'Cleverness?' she sniffed. 'Look where it gets you! I'll wager there's enough cleverness here to sink London Bridge! Brains? Give you a farthing for 'em!'

Then she settled down with a great commotion of her bonnet and shawl and began to talk of the changes for the worse in Vine Street since Smith had gone. Mr Mansfield, it seemed, hardly had a civil word for anybody and the mistress was a regular demon, finding fault where there was none . . . which Meg considered was a demon's chief office. Even handsome Mr Billing wasn't particularly welcome for, try as he might to be cheerful of an evening, the talk always came back to Smith; and there was an end of all cheerfulness. Meg said this with some satisfaction, as if it ought to've been a real comfort to Smith to learn he was the cause of misery.

But Smith nodded and smiled and bided his time. Then, at last, through all the byways of her conversation, Meg came back to 'You pore thing!' with the sigh of someone who's been the long way round.

Smith said: 'They're a-going to hang me, Meg.'

'Oh, you pore thing!'

'There's but one soul who can save me, Meg.'

'Ah! The master!'

'No, Meg. You!'

Meg looked astonished, fidgeted with the fringe of her shawl, then slowly shook her head with an air of great sadness.

'If heart can save you, child – then it's done. But this is a wicked world of cleverness . . .'

'It's heart I need, Meg – for it's cleverness what put me 'ere!'

Meg nodded deeply. That was no less than the truth.

'Say on, little one.'

So Smith bent close and began to mutter urgently and pleadingly in Meg's large, gentle ear.

Did she recall the paper she'd found when he'd been washed? She nodded.

Was it still where she'd put it?

Most likely . . . most likely, for it had been deep in a drawer.

Could she get at it?

Most likely –

Would she get at it – for Smith?

She opened her eyes in alarm. 'Why, child, it's the master's!'

'No! It was mine! And it's the only thing that'll save me.'

'I – I couldn't steal from the master.'

'But it was mine –'

'It's all a nasty piece of cleverness, child! You'd be best off without it! Believe Meg!'

'Meg – Meg! You're a-hanging me! True as we're 'ere! If I don't get it, I'll be buried afore the spring! Meg –'

'Oh, little one . . . Oh . . .'

The frightened Meg had begun to cry with the sudden misery of her dilemma. Her heart and conscience were much at odds. More than ever, she hated cleverness and all it brought in its sly train.

'I – I don't know what to do. Oh Lord! What would me mother have said?'

As she rocked herself to and fro, the old man began to rock himself likewise – and then croaked, amazingly like the parrot he so closely resembled: 'Meg! Meg! Follow your 'eart, Meg!'

She looked startled – then stared with wet eyes at the disreputable old man. She nodded.

'That's her voice, child, and them's her words. She often talks to me now she's dead and gone. Sometimes out of old men, sometimes out of mischievous urchins – and sometimes out of heaps of potato peelings! And it's always, "Follow your heart, Meg." So I'll fetch you the paper, little Smith, and may it save yore poor neck from the shameful noose!'

Smith considered himself as good as out of the gaol and the change in him was as astonishing as it was abrupt. His spirits rose and he put on a confident, almost patronizing air. He strutted importantly about the dismal Stone Hall, even finding opportunities to practise his reading upon the scratched messages, prayers and rages that scarred the damp walls. God have mercy on me, he read out; and shrugged his shoulders. Next, he read, Jo loves Bess. He scratched his head and wondered why anybody should want to write such a thing on a prison wall. Then, God rot all lawyers. Hm! That was more like it!

His high spirits were bewildering to his sisters – who'd last seen him in the depths of gloom.

'Oh, Smut!' said Miss Fanny. 'To see you in such spirits is better than a pint of gin, dear. Now, no matter what befalls, we'll know you went happy!'

'Oh, I'll be 'appy going!' said Smith, enigmatically; and Miss Bridget stared at him sadly, as if he was a lost soul.

But Mr Billing understood. Maybe at first he wondered if Smith had the document already . . . for he'd arrived shortly after Meg had left. Not that it was really likely he'd seen her – there being such a stew in Newgate at that time, what with Mulrone's visitors and the bad weather – but he saw the bundle and smiled knowingly. Smith, seeing this look, divined its meaning. He shook his head and grinned.

'Not yet, Mister Billing. But it won't be long before the chimney-sweep down the road'll be situated to buy himself new brooms and a whole new chimney for his very own! If you take my meaning, Mister Billing.'

Mr Billing took his meaning.

'And it won't be long before a certain little bird flies out of its stone cage, eh, lad?' He beamed and laid his hand on Smith's thin shoulder.

'How much better it is to put our cards on the table – play fair – and be friends. Oh, the world's not such a bad place after all – for the likes of you and me!'

This was on Sunday, January fifteenth: a day remembered, if for no other reason than for the extraordinary violence and passion of its snow-storm. It was as if the Devil's cat had got among the angels and was scattering their feathers everywhere. There seemed no end to the snow . . .

Chapter 12

The snow continued to fall . . . sometimes in great whirling quantities, and sometimes – for half a day at a stretch – in idle, drifting flakes that wafted wearily down as if the air was filled with invisible obstructions, then added themselves imperceptibly to the general whiteness below.

The worn old streets were gone; the blackened roof-tiles were gone; the mournful chimneys and the dirty posts wore high white hats – and the houses themselves seemed to float, muffled, in a sea of white. Never, in all its life, had the Town looked so clean; it shamed the very sky, which was of a dirty, yellowish grey.

The business of the Town was slow and tedious: carriages and chairs crawled along where they supposed the streets to be like huge, tottery snails, bearing snow houses on their backs and leaving wet black trails to mark their passing. Even the nimble pie-men capered silently, sometimes slipped and lost their smoking trays so that half a hundred hot pies burned into the snow and pitted it like a black pox.

Visitors to Newgate Gaol were few and far between. Only the loving and hardy called. Dick Mulrone's friends were much diminished and it was said he grew scornful and sour and melancholy. Smith, waiting on Meg, grew uneasy; there was no snow inside of Newgate, so the travelling troubles of the world seemed as remote as the stars. Only his sisters and the ever-faithful Mr Billing came to see him and, once in a while, Lord Tom. In these days Lord Tom spent a deal of time with his doomed colleague, whose room, being less crowded, offered more space for Lord Tom to be noticed and welcomed. After which, smelling strongly of wine and with a kind of swaggering stagger, the green-cloaked high toby would look in briefly on Smith and give him the news of 'glorious Dick'.

'He's hopes,' said Lord Tom, with a mournful grin, 'of the snow piling so high under the Tree that, when the cart drives off, he'll be left standing instead of the horrible swing!'

Smith nodded, and was not above being grateful for his friend's efforts to be companionable. Then his abstracted air returned as he tried hard to imagine what was preventing Meg.

There was now little time left; Thursday came and went without a sniff of her. Smith feared Mr Billing would wax suspicious and impatient. But he never did and always contrived to remain amiable. Sometimes, though, Smith fancied he detected a curiously calculating air behind the attorney's good-will: as if he was not going to commit himself, heart and soul, till he knew the outcome of some other event. And it was on the Thursday that this abstraction of Mr Billing's became most plain. He was almost agitated . . . but still cautious not to offend. When he went, he left a more than ordinarily puzzled Smith.

But on the Friday Mr Billing came to Smith with a rueful and disarming smile which Smith returned with a look of such deep and earnest hope that stonier hearts than Mr Billing's (if any there were) would have been melted by it. He shook his head and laughed and murmured something about 'Smith's winning', and 'friendship coming before all'. Then he sat down and, to Smith's amazement, relief and delight, confided the plan for the escape.

Not long before, there'd been set up on Newgate's roof a great windmill with vanes a full twenty feet across. Its purpose was to purify the air. As it turned, it drew (by natural suction and skilful design), through tubes and tunnels joining into a middle shaft, much of the foul and pestilential vapours of the gaol. So? The ventilators! The grated apertures in the walls. The narrow tunnels that led, through dark and angled ways, to the great shaft that rose up to the windmill on the roof. From which grimy eminence, it was but a hop, a jump and a scramble to the nestage of adjoining roofs.

With beating heart and glittering eyes, Smith listened as the attorney muttered rapidly on. Dipping his finger fastidiously in Smith's ale he drew on the table-top a plan of the wards and halls of the gaol alongside which the ventages ran. Very narrow were the lower tunnels – wide enough only to admit a thin child. But on the next floor they were somewhat more spacious and roughly bricked so's to afford finger- and toe-holds for 'little birds to reach the sky'.

Wider and wider grew these tunnels, till at last they came into the main shaft that rose to the windmill and the heavens. Upward, always upward, must the little bird go, else he'd find himself in another cage!

Mr Billing carefully wiped his finger on his handkerchief and Smith stared at the shining lines and squares that were beginning to dry and lose their powerful meaning. But they were already well fixed in his mind. He nodded and looked up for the last question. When was he to go? Not yet. Why? The grating was not yet unlocked. The good offices of a certain gentleman (here, Mr Billing looked about him quickly) were not yet bespoke. But, never fear, they would be. When? On the Tuesday. Why so long? Not so long, only four more days. But why not Monday? Ah! Tuesday would be a day of great commotion. Dick Mulrone would be setting forth. Gaolers and turnkeys would be busied in keeping order – and too busy to notice a little bird fly out of its cage! Tuesday, at six o'clock, before Smith would have been moved to the sessions house for his trial. Tuesday: freedom day! Mr Billing grinned: document day!

Smith's wavering spirits lifted and he stared long and hard at the ventilator grating that was let into the wall beside the fireplace. But even now it was impossible to rid himself of a thousand uncanny fears of disasters pouncing before the Tuesday. Yet Mr Billing had been confident – and Mr Billing was nobody's fool. All that remained, then, was the visit from Meg with the document. Surely she'd not fail him! Not Meg with her monstrous great heart!

She didn't fail him. Or, at least, not entirely. She came on the following day. Her shawl, bonnet, skirts and shoes were loaded with snow. She'd walked the whole way and the effort had made her steam, so that there was a general meltingness about her. Her hair, eyebrows, nose and chin all seemed to be discharging water, which gave her red face a curiously dismayed air.

'A glass of gin, Meg?' said Smith anxiously, as she dripped into the tap-room.

She shivered and shook her head . . . and seemed unwilling to sit down. Suddenly, Smith – with a dreadful fear – saw that her dismay was more than snow deep. Her customarily round face was oval and her eyes were unnaturally red.

'Have you – have you got it, Meg?'

She stared at him in terrified sorrow – as if imploring him to hold his peace.

'Meg! Where is it?'

'Oh, child! Oh, little one! They'll hang you now for sure, and bury you afore the spring! Oh, you pore thing!'

'Meg! Where is it?'

'Heart weren't enough, little one. Horrible cleverness is all. Brains? Lord! I wish I had 'em!'

'*Where is it*?'

She dabbed at her nose with her sleeve and her whole face grew veiled with fearful memories.

'On Thursday . . . yes, the Thursday, the master and mistress went out together; so I took me chance, little one, and crept like a mouse to the study . . .'

Smith, the first shock of dread spent, listened in a sick dismay. What had gone so grievously awry?

'I was in the very room, child – the very room –' She repeated herself, as if to prove her heart had ever been twice as strong as any circumstance. '– When I heard a noise, child, from upstairs. From upstairs where you used to sleep. Oh Lord, dear! I thought – I feared you'd lost patience and gone from the gaol and come back on your own desperate account. I was worried half out of my mind! I thought of calling out to you . . . then I thought it'd frighten you off. So, quiet as a mouse, I crept out and went up them dreadful stairs. Sure enough, there was a noise coming from your own dear room. But queer noise: scraping – dragging – pulling – panting . . . like it was being torn apart by dumb beasts. Lord! Lord! I was that frightened! I thought maybe a bear had got in!'

'*What was it, Meg?*' whispered Smith – though maybe he had already guessed . . .

'I screamed, child! That I did! Screamed and shrieked till Vine Street echoed. I got a good pair of lungs, child – a good pair of lungs.'

'And – then?'

'It must have scared 'em!'

'Who?'

'Two horrible men in brown! They burst out of the room in a terrible rage! I thought they'd kill me – but they rushed past me and down the stairs, then out through the front door like the wind o' hell!'

'The Thursday? This was on – on the Thursday, Meg?'

Meg stared at him vaguely, wondering why the day should have mattered so much. But among all the wild and panic-stricken thoughts that had whirled through Smith's head, one had stuck fast. On the day following that Thursday (when the attorney had been so agitated), Mr Billing had come to him with a rueful smile – a smile that Smith knew now was of disappointment. And he'd said Smith had won. Indeed, he'd won! The men in brown had failed.

'So there's no more hope, little one,' said Meg at last, with the grandmother of all sighs.

'No more hope?'

Smith looked at her, bewildered – having missed the chief part of her bad news. With a groan she repeated it. The burglary had so alarmed Mr Mansfield that he'd locked all his papers securely away. There was now no hope in the world of getting at them.

'Oh, child! They'll hang you now, and Meg, heart and all, won't be able to stop 'em! Why, child – you're a-smiling! Why, Smith, dear – you ain't down-hearted! Oh, God bless you, dear, for not breaking Meg's heart with your despairing. You'll go straight to heaven, Smith – no matter *what* you done!'

Smith, in spite of the evil news, was smiling in the most strangely excited way; and when at last she went, promising that she'd try to do something, no matter what, to save him, he called loudly after her: 'Thank you, Meg! Truly, thank you! You've saved me life!' Which was like Sunday bells in her ears!

Even the old man had been surprised, and he'd thought himself long past such sensations. But Smith, saying nothing, grinned most knowingly. Aggravated, the old man shuffled close beside him.

'You've not got it yet, have you?'

'No. I ain't. But nor has he!'

'So what are you grinning for? And why did you thank that sloppy baggage?'

'Because that lawyer's got ears as long as Watling Street – and I'd like him to think I'm pleased!'

The old man chuckled. No matter what the cause, he enjoyed folk being misled.

'He thought he'd have me for 'is dinner,' went on Smith, his face darkening with contempt. 'He thought I was that easy. Oh! That crafty lawyer, him!'

The old man grinned. He liked to hear of scoundrelly behaviour. Very satisfying he found it.

'And his friends in brown! Wish I'd seen their faces! Wish I'd seen *his* face when they told him what luck they'd had!'

The old man agreed. *He'd* liked to have seen such a multiplication of dismay. He enjoyed dismay.

'And picture his oily face now – when 'e hears simple little Smith has just thanked Meg 'eartily! "Tom Billing," he'll say to himself, "you got to help that lad. It stands to reason he's got the document already. Else why did he thank that sloppy baggage?" Oh yes! Picture 'is face!'

The old man pictured it and seemed to enjoy that most of all. The two of them – the old man not much bigger than Smith – sat grinning at each other across the mournful fireplace like a pair of goblin fire-dogs.

'Won't be long now,' said the old man, jerking his head towards the ventilator; and Smith felt an odd pang of regret – even shame – that he'd be escaping and the old man would not. But the old man didn't seem to mind. Indeed, he seemed quite gay at the thought for, though there were many things he liked much better, he was quite partial to the idea of the occasional little bird flying off.

Not that there was any remarkable sympathy between these two strongly differing prisoners, or even any mysterious bond of friendship. There was nothing in common between them save the fireplace, and even there each maintained his own side and scowled pretty formidably if there was any encroachment by the other.

'What d'you want? A whole bleeding park?' the offended one would mutter; and the trespasser would sniff and move back again. Then there'd be silence between them for several minutes while they watched the fierce and dingy residents of the Stone Hall going about their endless, purposeless business.

God knows what the old man thought as he gazed at his eternal neighbours to whom each day was as a year (with but a single season) and yesterday was a thousand years gone and of no more account. He must have had some thoughts – for every man has thoughts, be they never so dark – but maybe they were too awkward for words, like the prints left by a bird in the sky.

Even Smith's thoughts were vague and shifting. The anticipation of escaping gave him both a superior feeling towards those who could not – and a queer affection. His time among them, he was firmly convinced, could now be counted in hours.

Then something happened on the Monday evening that frightened the wits out of him and filled those last hours with commotion and dread.

'Visitor!' croaked the old man, sharpishly. 'Look lively! Visitor!'

Smith looked up – and was at once struck with astonishment and apprehension. The visitor was Miss Mansfield!

A terrible feeling that Mr Billing had confided the plan to Miss Mansfield and she, in a righteous rage, had come to wreck it, chilled his heart. He could conceive of no other reason. His eyes glittered desperately.

'Smith!' cried Miss Mansfield, throwing back her hood and staring about her in horror and shame. 'You've grown vastly dirty again!'

'Mister Jones won't mind –'

'Who's he?'

'The 'angman!'

Impulsively, Miss Mansfield knelt down and stretched out her arms (careless of her cloak, whose yellow lining flashed out, abrupt as a flower), and took Smith's shoulders.

'Keep off! Keep off!' he cried fearfully – with black memories of his last day in Vine Street and a feeling that Miss Mansfield was come on a worse errand than to tell him he was dirty. This feeling was exceedingly strong and set up a shivering through all his thin body.

Miss Mansfield scowled ferociously, and tried to blink away her tears. She turned to the old man who was watching with abiding interest.

'I – I would help him –'

'He don't need your help, ma'am.'

'What d'you want with me? Keep off! Leave me alone! I hate you!' almost screeched Smith in his fright.

The pain that he was inflicting was out of all proportion to his small size. His revenge on the Saint of Vine Street – did he but know it – was complete indeed. The lady's face had so distraught and tormented an aspect that even the sneering watchers were struck by it. Though she'd come to the gaol to tell Smith something, she could not overcome her own distress sufficiently to say more than: 'Smith . . . child . . . I – I would help . . . Don't hate us, I beg of you! Smith – Smith –'

But Smith glared and glared, morbidly convinced that the mad daughter of the mad father was come as harbinger of doom.

Which, in a way, she was. Suddenly there was a disturbance at the other end of the hall. Turnkeys were shouting; the seething, irritable crowd was being pushed and chivvied. It moved this way and that, till at last it parted and fell away somewhat savagely from a tremendous figure who'd been caught in its midst, despite the turnkeys who'd been beating at the felons and debtors and shouting:

'Blind man! Blind man! Make way –'

It was Mr Mansfield, blind as night, helplessly upright, his black spectacles in the great gloom looking more than ever like deep holes in his head. The turnkeys pushed obstructions from his path and led him, with many an important scowl at the resentful crowd, towards the fireplace.

Miss Mansfield looked alarmed and angry. She'd left her father in the carriage; bade him not come in, said she'd accomplish all without interference or help ... So why *had* he come, with that strange, desperate look about his mouth that disturbed her violently?

'Daughter –'

'Yes, sir –'

The blind man nodded and seemed to stare at the wall, as if, even to his useless eyes, the horror, darkness, degradation and shame of the Stone Hall was a sight not to be endured.

'Is – he – here?'

'Yes, sir.'

'Smith,' said Mr Mansfield, quietly. 'Do you know what this is?'

He thrust his hand into his coat and drew out – *the document*!

A sound between a scream and a groan told Mr Mansfield that Smith knew.

'Meg told us,' murmured Miss Mansfield. 'In tears, she came – poor soul! She was at her wits' end, and said it was the only thing that would save you . . .'

'Do you know what it is, Smith?'

'No! No! Never seen it before!'

'Look again. Look closely. Look hard.'

Helplessly, Smith looked. Yellower and more stained than he remembered – smaller, even – but it was the document. Now he could read on the outside: *To Mr Lennard. Billing and Lennard of Curtis Court, Godliman Street*.

Frantically his eyes strove to pierce the fold in the paper and read what was within, but in vain. He had a mad idea of snatching it. But where could he fly? Up the chimney?

'Never – seen – it – before!' he repeated, but his voice was harsh and unequal.

Mr Mansfield put the paper away and Smith's eyes followed it, into the vital pocket where all was black as night.

'Mr Lennard is at Prickler's Hill. I'm taking this document to him, Smith.'

'W-what's in it, then?'

'I – I do not know. It is for Mr Lennard. A dead man's wish, Smith. Binding. No arguing with it. It shall be delivered. Tomorrow.'

'And let's hope and pray, Smith,' said Miss Mansfield, still kneeling, 'that it will indeed save you –'

'Tomorrow,' went on Mr Mansfield, 'Mr Billing will apply for an adjournment of your trial. I have asked him–'

'Then *he* knows?' This was meant for a whisper, but it came out very near a scream.

'He knows no more than I've told him. Why should he? This is Mr Lennard's affair –'

'He knows – he knows!' moaned Smith, now in blackest despair, for it seemed to him that the evil document was coming full circle. He knew for certain that blind Mr Mansfield was as marked and doomed a soul as had been Mr Field.

All Smith's hatred and feelings of revenge sank abruptly in a sea of pity. The two men in brown would waylay the magistrate and murder him. And so at last they'd have what they'd been paid to get; and maybe Mr Black would thank them in his soft voice . . . In his mind's eye Smith could already see the look on Mr Mansfield's face as his soul left his body; and it was the self-same look he'd seen in Curtis Court.

'You blind old fool!' he wept furiously. 'They'll kill you! You old madman! Blind, blind, blind right through you are!'

But Mr Mansfield and his daughter were already moving, and the turnkeys were clearing their path. Men stared at the blind Justice hostilely, shook their fists at him, made threatening faces – and sometimes jeered. Someone managed to push his foot out so that the blind man staggered and nearly fell; but his daughter gripped hold on his arm and steadied him – in body, if not in spirit.

When they were gone, Smith looked dismally about for a certain fish-eyed gaoler who, he had reason to believe, was the one who retailed everything to Mr Billing and had most likely been paid to unlock the grating. His heart quickened. The man was nowhere to be seen. He had not been present. Was it still possible, then, that the escape would go forward? That the gaoler would do what he'd been paid for without further reference to his employer? Or had Mr Billing, knowing what he knew, already summoned him and grimly shaken his head? Scarce eighteen hours remained . . .

Chapter 13

It was a strange night, much given over to restlessness and rumours about Dick Mulrone. Rumours that he'd nubbed himself to cheat Mr Jones; rumours that he'd been reprieved and was dead drunk on that score; rumours that he'd changed clothes with a visitor and gone out as the Duchess of Newcastle; rumours that twenty of his roistering friends had broke in, armed with pistols, muskets and poniards, to whisk him back to the freedom of Hounslow Heath where coaches lumbered in their dozens, over-ripe for the plucking . . .

Then, between midnight and dawn, the easy voice of Mr Jones, the hangman, put a stop to it all:

'On the last day of counting
My true love sent to me:
Twelve jurors juggling,
Eleven clerks a-counting
Ten friends a-failing,
Nine dead men . . .
Eight widows weeping,
Seven judges judging,
Six drummers drumming,
Five yards of rope . . .
Four sextons digging,
Three parsons praying,
Two horses drawing –
And a felon in an elm tree.'

'That's my boy!' mumbled the old man – and leaned over to dig his companion in the ribs. But Smith had at last gone to sleep, so the old man desisted and rocked himself to and fro, humming the tune of the Tyburn Carol as softly as a lullaby, and gently clinking his fetters in time, so that the tune and the jingling might have sounded like Christmas harness in a dreaming ear.

At a quarter to six – or thereabouts – the old man shook Smith and bade him be gone.

The Stone Hall was dark and quiet, still – as a consequence of the disturbed night. Probably no one was awake save the old man and the furtive boy.

'Up on me back!' breathed the old man and knelt so's Smith might mount on that bony eminence to reach the grating.

'What if it ain't unlocked?' whispered Smith, full of last minute dreads and alarms.

'It's been done.'

'When?'

'While you slept. I heard. I saw. Come, now – up! Up! Up!'

Smith paused. 'D'you think you could come too?'

'Don't want to. This is me home. Got company.'

Smith nodded. He shook the old man's hand.

'I'll not be seeing you more –'

'I hopes not! Up you go!'

Smith hoisted himself on the old man's back, which was as hard and steady as a rock.

'Hope you gets a gentleman for the fireplace what suits –'

'That's my affair!'

'No offence –'

'None took. In you go, you scabby little sparrow!'

Smith had opened the grating. The air within was thick and damp and laden with evil smells. For a moment he thought the vent was too narrow even for him. Then he pushed with his feet against the old man's back and felt, first his shoulders, then his arms, elbows and hips scrape the rough stone walls.

'You're in!' he heard the old man whisper. 'Best of luck – and watch out for –'

Smith never heard what he was to watch out for, as all sound behind him was lost in the eerie sighing of the prison's secret lungs.

This sighing was as regular as breathing itself – and a thousand times more foul for, high up on the roof, the windmill was motionless, under a muffling blockage of snow.

A hundred and fifty feet of rough, uncanny darkness, divided into three steep channels, lay between Smith and the last great shaft. At the juncture of each of these channels, once jagged but now smooth and somewhat slippery apertures were let in; these led to other parts of the gaol and furnished Smith with foot- and finger-holds to heave himself round each sharp bend and continue his upward burrowing. That he *was* moving upward, he knew chiefly by the direction of his own sweat which ran continually into his eyes . . . not that those organs were of much use, for the darkness was formidable and absolute.

'So what was I to watch out for?' he muttered, ironically. 'Black rats? Black cats?'

The sound of his own voice cheered him . . . and henceforward he mocked his trembling spirits aloud: with a curious effect of which he had no knowledge. His mumbling, muttering tones travelled weirdly through devious passages and stony veins till they were wafted into the deepest and most dreadful parts of the gaol.

A man in the Press-Room – on whom were weights past bearing – heard faintly:

'Come on, now, me boy! Give in! Not you, me sweeting! What's a bruised belly between friends? On with you! Up with you – to the waiting heavens!'

But other gaol-birds in their remote cages heard, maybe, nothing so apt and heartening. Curses and abuse of the prison's scope and architecture came out of the various gratings – as if Newgate were alive to its own wretchedness and was at last complaining aloud. Then (in the King's Bench Ward), 'Be off with you! You fat, wicked 'orror! What are you waiting for? Dinner? Be off or I'll bite your 'orrible 'ead off!'

Smith and a rat. He'd met it by a nest of vents, its eyes gleaming in some vague, wandering light. It had come from a deeper channel and now stopped, amazed to watch what it took to be a grand relation, passing bulkily by.

'Upways, downways, in me lady's chamber! Which way now? Lost! "Up," he said. But which way's up? Where's the sky? Which of these dismal ways is the one to 'eaven? Come, me old friend! Try this fair stinker! Feet first – as they says in the trade!'

This, heard in My Lady's Hold, caused much terror and consternation; but farther on the wandering voice (believed by some to be that of a stoned-up ghost) was not so gay. It complained horribly of bruises and swellings got from scrapes and pressures against the ragged, bulging walls. It complained of having taken a wrong turn and finding itself, baffled and helpless, staring through bars into a cage more desolate than the one that had been left. It seemed to be losing heart under the strain of an intolerable journey. So miserable did the voice become at this point, that those who heard it were moved almost to tears by a plight they had no notion of, and whispered: 'Whatever you are – wherever you are – for God's sake cheer up – and the best of luck!'

Maybe this had reached its mark? At all events, nothing more was heard of the travelling voice, and the iron-barred vents were as silent as the grave.

What had happened? Smith had come into the last great shaft: the broad-ribbed, secret gullet that led to the windmill and the sky.

Bruised and much fouled from his journeying, he crouched in the last bend and stared triumphantly up. Fifteen feet above him hung the motionless vanes of the windmill, folded in snow. Beyond was the sky: grey and weighty and still dispensing its flakes which flickered down and down and down – even kissing Smith's upturned face.

A tremendous moment. Not even the Dean of St Paul's had as fine a view to heaven, nor a more heartfelt gaze at the sky. Smith began to climb . . .

He stopped. There was an oddness about the lip of the shaft. A ragged irregularity, which seemed to be growing subtly. Two swellings . . .

A sudden gust of wind whipped a veil of snow

across his vision; then it was gone and the two swellings were most marked.

What were they? Heads. Two men. A pair of hands reached down. Fingers twitched and beckoned . . .

In the sudden and terrible agony of his betrayal, Smith screamed aloud! Looking down upon him, waiting for him, grinning at him, were the two men in brown!

There came a second gust of wind, which performed a curious office. Or it might have been the effect of the amazed and horrified child's scream . . . for sudden noises of a certain pitch sometimes have the power of a giant's hand.

A quantity of snow shook and fell from the mechanism of the windmill, which now began to turn and draw up the air into the shaft, thus setting into motion all the stagnant, thick and heavy vapours that lay in the deep, stone veins of the gaol. Up they came, blundering into the churning mill.

But this was not all. A second, more fearful circumstance attended. An uproar – as if the lid of hell itself had been lifted – filled the shaft and shrieked and jabbered to the sky!

Together with the air, there had been sucked up from the gratings – through every portage and vent – the furious and savage voices of the gaol's inhabitants. Groans from the Press-Room, curses from the Stone Hall, hard, high laughter from the Master Debtors, and shrieks and wild whisperings from holds and wards and cells unknown – all mingled together in a chorus of truly monstrous scope and dimensions.

Fearfully, the men in brown stared at one another. Then they recalled their purpose. They looked down and added their own curses to the dreadful torrent. The boy was gone!

Smith, choked, deafened and despairing, had let go his hold. Eight feet he'd thumped to the bottom of the shaft. Then, his force not spent, he'd slipped, squealing, down a hole of formidable steepness – a vent that led, God knew where!

Had Smith been brought up to the Church, he'd have had a prayer off pat – for he travelled at speed on what he was sure was his last journey. (But, if he'd been brought up to the Church, he'd most likely not have been falling down a ventilator in Newgate Gaol!)

'Gawd!' he panted. 'Watch out – for 'ere comes Smith!'

Then – from some seven feet above the floor,

between the pulpit and the open pews of the prison chapel – shot out a dusty, dirty bundle of commotion that howled as it fell, picked itself up – and bolted directly for the door.

Smith was back in gaol.

The chapel was empty; but outside its door was a regular hubbub. The last sermon had just been preached over Dick Mulrone. He was on his way to the hangman's cart. All of his friends, all of his admirers, all of his well-wishers had come to watch him – and now crowded the passages for a last pat on the back and a last sad wave.

The crowd was tremendous – more than enough to engulf the scurrying Smith. On all fours, he went among skirts and legs that were like a trampling forest.

'Got to get out! Got to get out!' he muttered – and butted and bit his way along. He came to a corner at the head of some stairs and was momentarily free –

'Smut!' shrieked a voice. 'It's Smut!'

His sisters! Come to attend his trial; but had been first dragged by Lord Tom to see the last of the hero of Hounslow Heath. ('Give him a good send-off, m'dears. He'd have done as much for me.')

'Got to get out!' panted Smith, still on his hands

and knees and glaring up at his family as though he was their faithful mongrel hound.

'Oh, Smut!' cried Miss Fanny. 'You'll be took and ironed for this!'

'Quick!' whispered Miss Bridget, handsome in her Tuesday best. 'Under my skirt, child! Pop underneath – and not a sound!'

Miss Bridget tipped her great hoop so's her skirt rose like a monstrous black bell about to chime against the strongly pantalooned clappers that were her legs. Smith looked briefly at his elder sister – and grinned. He darted forward and Miss Bridget dropped her skirts.

So began Smith's escape from Newgate Gaol, not at all as he'd dreamed – nor certainly as had been planned for him – but rather a quiet, muffled exit through the great gate itself.

True, there were alarms on the way, and some discomforts. Smith found it hard to keep out of the way of Miss Bridget's feet – else *she* found it hard to prevent herself booting her felonious brother as if for his sins.

Miss Fanny also gave cause for alarm by asking aloud if 'little Smut was all right in his flannel nest?' till Miss Bridget was heard to declare aloud:

'You are a foolish cow, Fan! Hold your tongue, for pity's sake!'

Then Lord Tom joined them (Smith would have known those sturdy feet anywhere) and Miss Fanny couldn't resist whispering: 'We've got him safe and sound! You'll never guess where, Lord Tom! Not in a thousand years!'

But it seemed Miss Fanny ogled and stared and giggled so much at her sister's heaving skirt that Lord Tom guessed directly, but had the good sense to hold his peace and bid Miss Fanny to do likewise.

Then, at last, they were outside and beginning to walk away.

'Look! Look!' shrieked Miss Fanny, suddenly. 'Oh, Brid! Look!'

She pointed. Miss Bridget paled. Lord Tom looked alarmed.

In the thick snow behind Miss Bridget were not only her own footprints, but the unmistakable hop and scamper marks of an extra pair of feet!

'We'll walk behind you, Brid,' said Miss Fanny; and for the rest of that extraordinary journey, Miss Bridget had two of the most particular and devoted followers a lady could have wished for. They followed in all of her four footprints with a caution and respect most exemplary!

By the time they got to Turnmill Street it was hard on ten o'clock.

'Home, child!' whispered Miss Bridget – and raised her skirt a trifle to step across the familiar door of the Red Lion Tavern.

As she did so, there was a faint shouting and roaring that seemed to be coming from a long way off.

'What was that, Lord Tom?'

The highwayman sighed. 'From Tyburn, m'dear. They've just nubbed grand Dick Mulrone! I'm the only one left, Fanny. When will it be my turn?'

Chapter 14

If ever a man could tell, to the nearest five minutes, how long it would take a particular coach, leaving a particular part of the Town and going north, to come to the edge of Finchley Common, that man was Lord Tom. Not your fat rumbling trundler nor your light-slung gig, passing northward through the Town, was capable of keeping Lord Tom waiting upon his wild and lonely hunting ground. He knew their paces as well as his own and boasted famously that his prizes came, so to speak, by prompt appointment.

Indeed, it was said in the trade that Lord Tom might have made a better living by employing his genius in Town and auctioning his judgement for others to ride out for the 'stand and deliver'.

Not that he didn't ride well and shoot well, but it was sometimes said, by those who'd accompanied him, that his nature was too bold for so secret an undertaking and he was inclined to show courage when there was no call for it.

'Given the size of the coach – as you've described it – given this weather, given the crowds for Dick Mulrone this day, given the starting from Vine Street – your Mr Mansfield will take luncheon at the Queen's Head in Lamb's Conduit Fields and come upon the Common at half after four o'clock. 'Tis certain, Smut. Sure as we're in this cellar. Sure as my name's Lord Tom. At half after four. And at five –' He paused, his finger raised, like he was hailing a chair.

'At five, Lord Tom?'

'We'll have him!'

Miss Fanny looked at her friend admiringly, but Smith was yet doubtful.

'Ye-es, Lord Tom . . . if *someone else* don't have him first!' Lord Tom sighed and scratched his cheek – then examined the hand he'd employed.

'D'you mean our two friends in brown?'

Smith shivered – and nodded.

Said Miss Fanny: 'Lord Tom'll see them off, Smut. You'll see!'

And Lord Tom, with a mighty scowl, agreed.

'I'll blow blue daylight through 'em, Smut! There's never a man yet who's dared come 'tween Lord Tom and his lawful prize. You'll see 'em scamper, my lad!'

'And then – our dockiment, at last!'

'The document!' suddenly exclaimed Miss Bridget, bitterly. All this while, during the making and testing of the plan, she'd kept a resentful quiet; but now she could no more hold her peace.

'How I hate and despise it! For it's brought an old man to his death and made murderers of naught but common thieves. And now – and now it's turned our own poor mite, what has never sinned deeper than a passing pocket, into a dwarfish toby! To take such a child on to the murdering Common for to rob a blind man! Oh, for shame – shame – shame!'

Lord Tom chewed his lip and shook his head. He stood up with a clatter of iron-ware and began to pace the cellar.

'What would you have me do, Miss Bridget? In your own very hearing – not an hour ago – in this very residence I've a-pleaded with him; I've a-begged him; I've a-warned him and I've a-supplicated with him not to come. But that lad's determined. Nothing anyone can say will shake him. He's iron, Miss Bridget. He's steel. He's rock. He's a fixture, ma'am!'

Smith – who felt as far from any of these things as was imaginable – nodded vigorously.

Since he'd left the dreadful gaol in the vinegary, rustling blackness of his sister's skirt, with her legs coming and going like engines of destruction, he'd thought of nothing but Mr Mansfield with the fatal document on his way to Prickler's Hill. To say that nothing would have stopped Smith wasn't quite true. A knife in the ribs would have stopped him; likewise, a ball in the chest. But Lord Tom's warnings and Miss Bridget's respectable anger stood but a small chance against the furious urgings of his own heart and head.

Miss Fanny – to do her justice – must have seen this right from the start, for she never opposed her 'sweet Smut', but agreed 'our dockiment must come first'. Miss Bridget upbraided her, sneered at her, called her an 'avaricious slut'. But Miss Fanny only looked forgiving as her sister railed and put her arm round Smith's shoulders and declared: 'If his heart's in it, Brid dear, 'tis wicked to thwart him!'

So Miss Bridget turned the full force of her tongue upon Lord Tom, who was somewhat shaken by it; for he had, maybe, more prideful feelings than Miss Fanny. So the highwayman was driven to defend himself, and feel that he had to restore himself in the eyes of Miss Fanny and Smith.

Not that Miss Bridget's tempest could ever have sunk Lord Tom in Smith's bright eyes, for the boy held the green-cloaked robber in the deepest admiration and respect. Which respect, agreeably enough, was treasured up by Lord Tom as a bright warm day to remember in the winter of his life. With energy and dignity, he painted such a picture of his trade that only the coldest of hearts could have scorned.

'Gallantry, ma'am – there's gallantry on the Common! And fierce beauty and soaring adventure!'

The highwayman's eyes sparkled and he brushed the back of his hand across his cheek, as if he could feel the wild night upon it. Then he went on to relate exploits that he'd told of many times before – but never so handsomely. And he spoke of other famous gentlemen who'd once waited, hid and pounced where *he* now waited, hid and pounced: Duval ('Hanged!' snapped Miss Bridget), Turpin ('Hanged!'), Captain Robinson ('Hanged!').

'Yes, ma'am, they paid for their joys. They're dead and gone . . . and so've a great many other folk. 'Tis the common penalty for living. But it's not the quiet, mewing, moaning bed-perishings that haunt the Common of a moony night. No, ma'am! When we ride out, we ride with the great ghostly company of the nubbed! Many a time I've heard, "Lord Tom, Lord Tom – I'm a-watching you, friend," in Turpin's own voice!'

Then Lord Tom, with dreamy grandeur, told of these dead men's doings in the days of their lives – and then back to his own (to draw a parallel) – then back again . . . till it was hard to tell who'd done what: Duval, Robinson, Turpin – or Lord Tom.

In spite of herself, Miss Bridget's heart beat a little faster . . . for she was but three and twenty and Miss Fanny's and Smith's sister, when all was said and done.

Smith's heart, also, was beating faster – but from a strong anxiety that Lord Tom's eloquence was dangerously delaying them, and that they'd be too late upon the Common. For the first time in his life, he wished Lord Tom had had fewer adventures – and hadn't remembered them so well!

'By tonight, we'll have our dockiment safe and sound,' he heard Miss Fanny murmur. 'And Smut'll read it to us . . . with new tallows and we three sat at the table . . . for all the world, Brid, like reading a psalm from the Scriptures.'

The document: with a start, Smith remembered it. Not that he'd ever forgotten it, but its importance now seemed changed. If, by destroying the document, he could have destroyed Mr Black and his friends, he'd have done so. The document was now not so much a means of his going up in the world, but a way of preventing his going down.

'Well, Smut, me comrade-in-arms of this day! Are we fit and ready?' exclaimed Lord Tom at last, staring at a fine French watch that had been the subject of his last told adventure. 'Five minutes to make your adieus, Smut – then it's the Common for the pair of us!'

Thankfully, and with mounting excitement, Smith left his seat and stationed himself beside the tremendous highwayman, when Miss Bridget, somewhat desperately, protested: 'But he'll freeze to death! He cannot go so ill-dressed!'

There was a further delay, while an ancient cloak was found to cover Smith's bedraggled finery and a queer hat, that Miss Fanny had once toyed with, to cover his tangled and matted head.

He had a certain shabby splendour – and even Miss Bridget gazed at him with surprise and a reluctant admiration as he began to mount the stairs. Smith, caught up in the romantic spirit, felt himself full of the gallantest dreams. He turned, waved and cried: 'Adieu, dear ladies! Wish me –'

He stopped. There was a loud knock on the door.

'Gawd!' muttered Smith. 'It's for me!'

He bolted back into the cellar, his cloak flapping like ruined wings, and hid behind the curtain. Lord Tom stood, grandly guarding his small friend's sanctuary, and the two sisters rose together.

'Come in!'

There entered a small, wizened man with eager eyes, carrying a bundle. He peered down into the body of the cellar and grinned and nodded to the company. It was Mr Jones's assistant come, not for Smith, but with Dick Mulrone's fine suit. To be altered for Mr Jones's father. 'There's a good son for you!'

He threw the bundle on the table and said Mr Jones himself would be calling to describe his father's figure and shape: tomorrow. Today he was tired out. The crowds! The shouting! Fairly frayed him!

Then he went – and left behind a gloomy silence. If ever four souls and a cellar were haunted by the lack of a ghost, they were gathered now. A coat, a waistcoat and a pair of breeches: that was all there was of Dick Mulrone. No breath nor whisper of a ghost came into the Red Lion's cellar to quicken the four sad hearts, or stir the pitiful heap of clothing. The gallantest robber of the Hounslow Heath was as dead as mutton; not able, even, to haunt his own breeches.

Lord Tom bowed his head. Miss Fanny wept. Said Miss Bridget: 'Take care of him, Lord Tom. For my heart chills. Watch over little Smut.'

'I'll guard him, ma'am. With me very life I do assure you – while he's with Lord Tom, no danger will offer. I – I promise you, ma'am. Come, lad – away!'

With the best will in the world Lord Tom tried to be in good spirits on the way to Finchley Common; but the sadness lingered, and he kept falling into a silence as heavy as the glum sky. And Smith, whose dearest dream and brightest hope had come to pass – to be riding out on the snaffling lay with his hero, Lord Tom – was as melancholy as sin.

Sitting on the front of the highwayman's saddle he turned round, from time to time, and saw Lord Tom's great, bristling face, dark under his hat, much troubled . . .

So they rode on, this weirdly romantic, fantastic pair – the infant gaol-bird and the glowering highwayman – through the thick snow towards the famous place where Lord Tom and all of his hanged ghosts waited, hid – and pounced.

Chapter 15

The snow, which had held off for some three hours, began again in earnest at about four o'clock as the light was perishing from the sky and there came up to Bob's Inn on the steep of Highgate Hill, a most weary horse bearing a full-sized man and an under-sized boy.

'Is this the place, Lord Tom?'

'The very same.'

Bob's Inn, a pleasant, newly built structure with three parlours and rooms for seven gentlemen (three double and one single), sat about fifty yards northward from the top of Highgate Hill and commanded a spacious view of the southern fingers of Finchley Common, from which it was distant by about half a steep mile. Thus from the snug windows, not a curricle, gig or coach could venture on to the Common without being interestedly viewed. For the further entertainment of his customers, Mr Bob had provided a strong spy-glass (at sixpence a half-hour) and certain information that might be of service. Mr Bob's customers were high tobies to a man.

'Knew 'em all!' was Mr Bob's proud boast as he stood by the cheerful fire of an evening. 'Duval – Turpin – Robinson . . . many's the time they've sat about this very snug, drinking and laughing – and popping to the windows for a nifty look!' (This, not-withstanding the glum fact that Duval had been hanged eighty years before and Bob looked no more than forty.) 'Yes, indeed! Knew 'em all!'

He welcomed Lord Tom and grinned affectionately at Smith, whom he recognized as a 'brisk, bright and prosperous apprentice to the Trade'. He made a place for the highwayman and his apprentice by the fire and dispatched an evil-eyed potboy for 'jars of the best'.

'Nothing coming, nothing going,' he murmured, jerking his head to the windows that commanded the best view of the Common. 'Not our sort of weather, eh, Lord Tom? Many's the time – ah, many's the time – great Duval himself would curse the snow for muffling his pickings! Aye, and a-warming his backside where you're a-warming yours, friend!'

Lord Tom was handsomely thawing himself out – and fizzing and drizzling into the hearth. His caped coat, whited like a sepulchre, was now beginning to patch through the covering of snow into a wet green – like a lawn after winter. Likewise, Smith, buffeted and stung by the whirling snow, bruised beyond belief by the dreadful horse, began to come to himself and crack and thaw and ease himself into a furtive smile.

'There's a coach due, Bob, within –' (Lord Tom drew out his French watch which the landlord eyed merrily and murmured, 'Ah! we remember that one, eh?') '– within this half hour. From Town toward Barnet.'

'You know best, friend. You got a reputation. But it surprises me: yes, indeed. Must be powerful business to draw an equipage across this murderous white nothingness!'

'It is, Bob. It surely is.'

He winked at Smith – then raised his fingers warningly to his lips as the potboy returned with the ale.

Not fifty yards to the west of Bob's stood another inn – an ancient, tottery, smoky building, the speaking likeness of Smith's Red Lion. This was The Wrestlers. It seemed that Lord Tom had a little brief business there. He charged Smith to wait for him and not to stir from Mr Bob's parlour: under no circumstances.

Mr Bob nodded. Lord Tom wasn't to worry. His own stout person would go bail for the apprentice's not shifting till Lord Tom returned.

The highwayman thanked him – then turned to his apprentice: 'Watch out for the coach, Smut. Mr Bob'll show you where. Here's a sixpence, Bob. Let the lad watch through the spy-glass. Let him be a real high toby while I'm gone! Just for ten minutes, eh?'

He tossed a coin on the table, but Bob shook his greasy, good-natured head.

'Keep your money, friend. On a night like this I'm all for the warmth of kindness. The lad can watch for free. Duval would have liked that. Yes, sir, I can hear him say, "Bob! Let the lad watch for free!"'

'There, Smut,' said Lord Tom, with sudden pride. 'There's a small taste of our companionage. You're among friends!'

Then, with a quick wave, he opened the door and his place was took by a flurry of snow, as he strode across the invisible road to The Wrestlers.

'A grand fellow!' remarked Bob. 'One of the best!'

He eased himself into a seat close by Smith and prepared to unburden himself of all his superior memories for the amazement of a new pair of ears. But Smith was staring so fiercely and anxiously at the window that overlooked the approaches to the Common, that Bob, seeing his best tales might pass unheeded, took pity on the boy and pointed to where the spy-glass stood on the mantelshelf.

'Take it, lad. Go watch for the coach. And remember, through that self-same glass the proudest, sharpest, gallantest eyes these parts have ever known, once stared. May their brilliancy lighten your viewing. Go stand by the window . . . elbows on the still . . . left knee cocked on the seat. The very attitude of Turpin! Duval was a taller man. He always used to sit . . .'

The capacious-memoried landlord rambled on, following Smith from the fire to the window, obliging him by pulling out the spy-glass into all of its gilt sections – then standing to one side with the warming remark that Smith was 'the very image of Claude Duval as a lad!'

Smith, pleased in spite of his urgency, stared out into the gathering night . . . past the ghostly reflection of his own thin, fierce face, through the snow-filled air, on to the deep white world that sank and humped and valleyed and hillocked for many a quiet, mysterious mile. This was northward. Southward lay the Town, speckled and spotted with lights.

'D'you see that long, shadowy finger?' breathed Mr Bob. 'That's the road the coach'll come by . . . *if* it comes.'

Smith saw, and raised the spy-glass so's the landscape jumped amazingly close at hand. He saw bushes and trees creaking under their white fruit which, every once in a while, the wind would shift and cause to thump and shower down, adding more whiteness to the overburdened ground.

Then, distant even in the spy-glass, he saw a square black creature, with a pair of gleaming yellow eyes, tipping and lumbering in the wake of two horses.

'It's coming!' muttered Smith, triumphantly. 'Lord Tom had best be quick!'

He turned to the side window and swung the spy-glass towards The Wrestlers, to see if the romantic figure of the highwayman was yet come out and was leaning through the whirling weather.

It was amazing! So strong was the glass that Smith felt he could have touched the door and walls and poked his head through the parlour window to say: 'Make haste, Lord Tom! The coach is sighted! Hurry, good friend of mine. Get up off your chair and leave those –'

Those what? For there sat Lord Tom, large and near as life – leaning across a table, in deep discussion with . . .

Smith lowered the spy-glass abruptly and wiped the lens. Then he looked again. He grew pale. His skin began to prickle as if the air was full of thorns and arrows. His belly turned unquiet and he began to feel sick.

Lord Tom was in deep discussion with the two men in brown. Lord Tom. His strong friend, his champion, even his hero . . . Very fearful of face, was he: very cringing, very humble. (Yes, sirs! No, sirs! The bland man's as good as dead, sirs! And ain't I betrayed the lad neatly? Hope you're pleased with me, sir!)

Smith put down the glass.

'What's amiss, lad?'

'Nothing! You mind your own damned business, Mister Bob – and I'll mind mine!'

Smith spoke through his hands – which were before his face to hide his rushing tears.

A very black, bitter and tragic place was the world to Smith as he understood the scope of his friend's treachery. It was not Miss Fanny's prattling that had betrayed his whereabouts, but the whispers of gallant Lord Tom! The blind man's turning against him was as nothing to the wretchedness he now endured. Smith had been struck deep indeed.

'I'll fetch you a tot of brandy, lad!' murmured Bob, much concerned and believing the apprentice to be, so to speak, the victim of 'stagecoach fright'. 'That'll put fire into you for the "stand and deliver"!'

He was gone only for a second, but when he returned the door was banging open and the parlour was empty, save for a whirl of snow. The highwayman's apprentice was gone.

'Come back! Come back!' he bellowed – but the small, tumbling, hurtling figure that plunged down the hillside was fast vanishing – and heeded him not.

*

In places the snow lay two feet deep and Smith, to rise out of it, had to bound in a mighty, springing fashion – like a tremendous flea. Every now and then he'd strike on an unexpectedly shallow patch, so his feet, meeting resistance, would shoot him more powerfully than ever into the air – from which he'd fall and roll over and over in a whirl of white. Then up he'd scramble, wet and panting, to bound onward – till he fell again . . .

Such tracks as he made were almost instantly filled in after him, so that the effect of his progress was oddly supernatural. And all the while, in a harsh, sobbing voice, he'd plead and cajole and curse and beg his own despairing person to hurry, hurry, hurry!

Three devils were after him: two in brown – and one in green. But the snow kept flinging coldly suffocating arms about him – as if to hold him forever in its freezing bosom – and, as he rose, the very heavens seemed to beat him down again with their fluffy torrents. The whole huge universe was turned against him: the earth, the sky, the wind – even his own failing limbs which ached for nothing more than a bed in the dreadful loving snow.

But each time, there came up out of the hole he'd made in the ground, a small rebellious voice:

'Come on with you, Smith! You dozy weasel! Up! Up! What for did you come out of the 'ouse of bondage? To sink and perish in this great Fleet Ditch of common 'opelessness? Not bleeding likely!' And then, in tones which shook with bitterness, grief and contempt: 'So to hell with you, Lord Tom! For that's where you belongs!'

On which the indomitable figure of Smith would rise up out of the white, and fumble on.

Where to? The road the coach would take: the shadowy finger that Mr Bob had pointed to. But where was it? He stared about him. Whiteness everywhere. No landmark, no post – nothing!

Once more, a feeling of hopelessness gripped him. He looked back up the hill. Three small black figures were on their way . . . In a sudden rage, Smith stamped his foot and glared about him.

Not seventy yards off, lumbered the coach! Towards him! The road – he was on it!

The horses panted and dragged and steamed. The coachman, high up on his snow-capped black mountain, leaned forward, eyes fairly glued to the vague shadow which was all he could see of firm ground. He dared not look elsewhere; one false move might end in a drift and finish the vital journey then and there.

Smith scrambled aside; sank up to his knees in snow; crouched down. He wished to God he'd waited for Mr Bob's tot of brandy; for what parts of him the weather neglected to chill, fright did for wonderfully.

On came the coach, its yellow lamps leaping like alarmed eyes as it rocked perilously, all haste and commotion – yet soundless. The snow and the wind muffled all. It might have been a spectral equipage, already lost some way back and only its spirit persisting.

Now it was close enough for Smith to pick out the coachman's features – his one-time master in the Vine Street yard. He heard the horses thumping in the snow and the harness groan and creak in the angry singing of the air. Still he waited. The coach drew level . . .

A friendly gust of wind whipped and whirled and sent stinging flakes into the coachman's face and eyes. Smith moved quickly; he seized hold on the door; dragged it open –

'Who's there? Who is it?' Mr Mansfield's voice, angry and alarmed, was swallowed up in the wind.

Smith reached within. He clutched at a coat sleeve – a wrist – a hand – and pulled with all his might.

'My God! My God!'

Out heaved the blind man, falling with the tilt of the coach into the muffling snow.

'For God's sake, who is it? What d'you want with me?'

Smith, still holding tight, did not answer. Instead, he dragged him down into the drifts by the side of the road while the untenanted coach – its door swinging helpless, like a one-armed soldier's sleeve – quaked and jolted on.

Again the blind man cried out and Smith fixed his hand over the betraying mouth and, in a whisper no man could have recognized, breathed: 'Quiet – if you values yore life!'

Twenty yards on the coach rocked to a halt. It had been accosted and pistols pointed the way to the coachman's brains.

The wind whipped familiar voices back to where the snow was fast hiding Smith and his prisoner.

'The lousy coach is empty!'

'Thank the Lord!' (The coachman.)

'That boy of your'n – Lord piddling Tom! – he's beat us to it.'

'Friends!' (Lord piddling Tom.) 'I swear I did what I could –'

'Not enough – not enough! You should have slit his mean throat – you green windbag!'

'Friends – friends! How was I to know –'

'You swore you'd fix him!'

'And so I meant to! I swear it!'

'Swear it to Mr Black! If he gives you leave! You'll bleed for this!'

'No! No! They must be near at hand! Let's search!'

'In this great 'owling blizzard?'

'Yes – yes!'

'We've had experience afore! Your little rat near killed us once with chasing him!'

(Smith, in concealment, couldn't restrain a beam of pride.)

'Then what's to be done?'

'On to Mr Black in the morning. That's what.'

'But – but –'

'"But" to your heart's content, fat man. Yore day's done. You blotted yore book. Maybe with blood, eh?'

'The coach! The coach!'

While they'd been thus engaged, the coachman had taken advantage. He'd whipped his horses and yelled them into a frenzy. Already, the coach heaved and plunged on its way!

'Stop, you fool! Stop – or you're dead!' Lord Tom raised his pistol – aimed – and fired. A cry from ahead. The coachman, high up, clutched at his side and began to slip . . . then he seemed to recover himself partly . . . and was lost from sight behind a clump of trees. When the coach reappeared, still lumbering fast, there was nothing on the box but a heavy, jerking shape that, any moment, would fall by the wayside, unheeded.

Smith, in his excitement, had withdrawn his hand from the magistrate's mouth.

'Is he – is he – killed?' whispered Mr Mansfield.

Smith did not answer. Instead, with bitter, lonely eyes, he watched the three figures turn and begin their climb up the hill. Then he stood up, brushed the accumulated snow from the magistrate's shoulders and head, and pulled him to his feet.

Four miles to the north lay Prickler's Hill. Smith set his face in that direction and, with his hand firmly about the blind man's wrist, began to walk. And the snow came down like a disaster . . .

Chapter 16

They made poor progress: in two hours something less than three-quarters of a mile. Every once in a while the boy would turn his back to the weather and face the blind man, drawing him on and, at the same time, seeming to retreat under the impassive stare of the snow-stained face. For there was no doubt the blind man sensed the scrutiny of unseen eyes (or did he feel warm breath softening the bitter wind?) and, as was his old habit, emptied his face of all tell-tale expression . . . Then the boy would grunt and turn about – to plod on into the scourging snow.

Sometimes, when they passed among the heavily bandaged trees, the wind would dislodge snow from the lower branches so that it thumped down, knocking the breath out of the two travellers and forcing them to halt for recovery. Then the blind man would once more ask his guide who he was and why he'd saved him and was leading him through this huge and bitter night. Perhaps he knew? It was hard to say.

'Very well, then – speak . . . anything . . . anything at all. Or are you dumb? A fine pair – we two! One with no tongue to tell what he sees – and the other with no eyes to see what's worth the telling. A humorous pair! Well, then – if you won't speak, sing!'

But Smith uttered never a word. He was deeply frightened of the magistrate's mania for justice. He dreaded that the blind man would give him up at the first opportunity. So let him think it's a perishing angel what's leading 'im, thought Smith and held his tongue.

At seven o'clock the snow began to abate – though the wind did not – and a great clearness and brilliancy settled upon the landscape, across which the boy and the blind man seemed to be the only moving things.

The magistrate, having worn out his conversation, turned to singing and chanting (maybe in the hope that his silent guide would join in and betray himself).

'"The Lord is my shepherd, I shall not want."'

You said it! thought Smith, plodding on.

'"He maketh me to lie down in green pastures –"'

You should see 'em! mouthed Smith with fierce irony. He blinked about him; the hills were white and the valleys were white, likewise the slopes between . . . The sky alone offered relief, being of a velvety blackness, pricked out with some fifteen or twenty frosty stars.

'"Thou preparest a table before me in the presence of mine enemies –"' Smith scowled through his windy tears for he'd not eaten that day.

The thought struck him that Mr Mansfield knew who he was all the time and was subtly mocking him – till the chance should offer of giving him up. Certainly, everything the blind man said seemed now to be cruelly humorous – and he said a great deal! Songs and poems and lumps of the Scriptures came puffing out of his mouth with much issue of smoking breath. This was Mr Mansfield's stock-in-trade – his vision of the world, seen through other men's eyes who'd digested their vision into words, and it made him a supper to last all his life.

His own memories of what the world looked like, he no longer trusted. He was a sensible man and knew full well the changes that must have been wrought since last he'd looked. His beloved daughter could no longer have been the fearful child caught in the fire he'd remembered for so long. Even the Town itself he knew to be much changed for everywhere he heard sounds of building and of tumbling and of men losing their way. Even Nature herself he suspected of ageing – and the wind and the cold seemed crueller than he recalled.

Maybe, even, they were breeding a new style of boy, now? He smiled – or tried to, but his cheeks were partly frozen. The child, Smith, for instance . . . He frowned as he recalled the powerful evidence against him. No. Whatever else might alter, justice remained fixed – like God Himself. Justice: the last refuge of a blind man.

Suddenly, he felt the grip on his wrist disappear. Frightened, he stopped, turning his face this way and that in the lonely wind. Had he been left? Oh God! Why?

Smith, beaten breathless by the weather – with a lock of his black hair (his hat was in Mr Bob's) frozen solid so's it banged against his forehead like a door-knocker, was suddenly attacked by common-sense. The old mole-in-the-hole was not changed. Stern and cold was his face – colder even than the snow that spotted it. Smith was not leading him; he was leading Smith – back into the horrible house of bondage! A thousand windy voices shouted in his ears, bidding him leave the old Justice and begone. The world was a freezing, lonely place. No one would give Smith quarter in it. Not his sisters, not his treacherous friend – and, least of all, the stern-faced magistrate. Not even the howling weather!

Further and further off backed Smith, amazed by his own madness in coming thus far. He stared at the stark, menacing form of the blind man with his stony heart.

Take, take, take! And never give naught in return! I'm done with you!

And then, as Smith watched, the blind man raised his hands. He turned about, tried to take a step, stumbled, recovered himself and cried out: 'Am I alone? Am I alone?'

His face, though much limited in expression by his shrouded eyes, was suddenly, and deeply, wretched. A desolate face, bespeaking a starved soul. That soul of his had been nourished on thin fare, these past twelve years, and it had grown weak without his knowing it, so that, when the wind blew, it bowed as if to break. And the wind blew as hard for the blind man as it did for the boy.

'You old blind Justice, you!' mumbled Smith, lurching back to Mr Mansfield. 'Give us your hand, then!'

The magistrate stretched out his hands, and nature made strange amends for a certain disability of his. Snow, dislodged from his spectacles and fallen against his eyes, had begun to melt so that the water trickled down his cheeks as if he was doing what he could not: weeping.

Bewildered, Smith gazed on Mr Mansfield's melting face. He took both the outstretched hands.

'Here – here, then. Both me hands. You ain't alone, Mister Mansfield – nor never was. I – I was only resting –'

'Smith – Smith – Smith!' cried the blind man, grasping in return the hands he'd never forgotten. 'Your voice at last! How I longed to hear it!'

'You knew it was me, then?'

'Yes – yes!'

'Then – why didn't you say?'

'You didn't want me to know, did you?'

'No. I was thinking you'd 'and me over to the Law.'

'And even so you came back?'

'I'm only a yewmanbeen.'

'*Only!*'

Smith freed one of Mr Mansfield's hands and turned once more into the weather.

'We'd best be moving – or we'll freeze in situation!'

They stumbled on a while longer – but no more in silence. A curious warmth seemed to have sprung up between them and rendered the wind less savage. Mr Mansfield told Smith that his daughter had stayed behind to attend his trial and to keep Mr Billing to his promise of the adjournment. It seemed it was she, the Saint of Vine Street, who'd kept her faith in Smith.

'Not you, Mister Mansfield?' asked Smith shrewdly.

'No, alas, not me. I'm no saint, Smith. Like you, I'm only a human being.'

'Queer, then, being an old mole-in-the-hole and helpless, you should come out in sich weather for . . . for what, Mister Mansfield? For the 'ealthy cold air?'

Mr Mansfield grinned awkwardly.

'That's it, Smith! For my health!'

Smith grinned back – then remembered his companion's disability and said: 'I'm a-smiling, Mister Mansfield!'

'Pleased to hear it, Smith.'

'You, too, Mister Mansfield. And a very cheering thing to see. You got a friendly smile, you know.'

'I didn't know, Smith. But now you've mentioned it, I'll take a special pride in it!'

And Mr Mansfield continued to smile into the icy wind in the firm hope that Smith would sometimes turn and get the benefit; which Smith did, always remembering to return the compliment aloud. Then he'd turn back again and chatter about what he could see and what he'd seen . . . describing his life and the doings of his sisters . . . and even his escape from the gaol. But he never mentioned Lord Tom nor any of the darkness that hemmed him in. Likewise, Mr Mansfield, though he confided in Smith much of his warmer past, said nothing of what must have lain deepest in both their thoughts – the murder of Mr Field.

Presently, they reached the top of a gentle slope.

'Cottage, Mister Mansfield . . . quarter mile off . . . light in the window . . . nice, snug little place. Looks warm. What say we knock on the door?'

'Don't mind if we do.'

Smith tucked his head as far as it would go into his collar and began the descent towards the cottage which lay in a snow-filled hollow.

A neat, well-built cottage, with good windows and a stout fence marking off its garden from the Common – though with the snow lying so heavy on garden and Common alike, the fence looked more peevish than necessary. There was a strong blossoming of smoke from the chimney that bespoke a warmer nature within than without . . . and the cottage's windows gleamed most cheerfully.

All this Smith described to Mr Mansfield, who nodded as they approached the door and said he was reminded of old fairy tales.

'A wood-chopper's cottage . . . an old wood-chopper and his brown-eyed wife –'

'Then there's money in chopping wood,' said Smith shrewdly. 'For there's a stable at the back and space for a carriage.'

He knocked on the door and Mr Mansfield

sighed as if he was almost sorry that their winter's journey – murderous as it had been – was ending in so ordinary and genteel a place.

The door opened an inch.

'Who's there? What d'you want?' The voice was harsh and irritable.

'Shelter!' cried Smith and Mr Mansfield together.

'Who for?'

'A blind man and a frozen child!'

'What was that?' came a woman's voice from within.

'Blind man and frozen child,' answered the first voice.

'Stuff and nonsense, Charlie!'

'That's what they said.'

'Have a look!'

The door opened farther to the full extent of its chain. A stout, waistcoated man, bald and frowning, peered out.

'Man and child, right enough, Mrs P.,' he called out.

'How big, Charlie?'

'Child's about – um – high as your chair and the man's taller than me.'

'Don't like it, Charlie.'

'No more do I. Shall I shut 'em out, Mrs P.?'

'Good God, sir!' exclaimed Mr Mansfield. 'In humanity's name! On such a night?'

'Did you hear that, Mrs P.? The weather, y'know!'

'Mrs P.!' shouted Smith. 'We're frozen near to death – and me friend's as blind as a post.'

'Charlie! See if he's blind!' came Mrs P.'s complaining voice. Obligingly, Mr Mansfield took off his spectacles and presented his face.

'Nasty,' said Charlie. 'Blind all right.'

'Then let 'em in, Charlie!' cried Mrs P. 'Keeping a blind man and a frozen child on your doorstep; ain't you got no humanity, sir? Oh, you're a weak vessel, Charlie Parkin!'

Thereupon, the chain was unfastened, the door opened wide and Smith and Mr Mansfield welcomed directly into the parlour.

'Hats! Coats! Boots!' shouted Mrs P. 'Quick, Charlie! Into the kitchen with 'em before we're drowned out again!'

'Least said, soonest mended,' said Charlie, collecting up those snowy articles, which were already dripping fast in the great heat of the parlour.

He bustled out and Mrs P. – a very small woman with sharp features and a blue cap – fixed Smith and Mr Mansfield on either side of the neat fire.

Indeed, everything about the parlour was neat: the cloth upon the table was neatly embroidered with neat little flowers, the plates upon that cloth were neat, and even the crumbs remaining on those plates had been neatly arranged, like soldiers drawn up for review.

'A very neat home,' said Smith to Mr Mansfield.

'You poor things!' said Mrs P., busy by the sideboard with glasses and some warming spirits. 'Lost your ways on the Common, I suppose?'

'Our coach was held up, ma'am,' said Mr Mansfield. 'Highwaymen.'

'Charlie!' shouted Mrs P. 'They was held up! Highwaymen!'

Instantly, Charlie reappeared, with a pistol in his hand. His eyes were fiery. 'Highwaymen? Where?'

'No, no! They' – she nodded to Smith and Mr Mansfield – 'was held up by highwaymen. Victims, Charlie. And come to us for succour.'

'Oh!' said Charlie, putting up his weapon. 'Them damned high tobies!'

'Fetch the book, Charlie.'

Charlie nodded, vanished back into the kitchen and reappeared with spectacles and a large ledger.

'Ink and fresh pen, Charlie.'

They were got from the sideboard.

'Brown paper, Charlie.'

This was to spread on the tablecloth to protect it from the consequences of Charlie's writings.

'Now, Charlie – off you go!'

Wonderingly, Smith watched and Mr Mansfield listened to these preparations.

'Blind man and boy,' said Mrs P. – and Charlie repeated it and slowly, which much help from his fumbling tongue, wrote it in the book.

'Held up – where was you held up?'

'On the Common, ma'am.'

'On the Common, Charlie.'

'On the Common, Mrs P. Two *Ms* and one *N*.'

'Robbed?'

'No, ma'am.'

'Not robbed, Charlie.'

Charlie wrote and Mrs P. sighed at her husband's slowness. ('A slow vessel, Mr Parkin.')

'Injured?'

'Our coachman was – murdered, I believe,' said Mr Mansfield, bleakly.

'Coachman murdered, Charlie.'

Charlie looked up and exchanged a long, deep stare with Mrs P. Then he shook his head. 'Them damned high tobies!'

Now Mrs P. came over with two glasses of spirits.

'Two measures of brandy, Charlie!' she called out as she offered them.

'Two measures of brandy,' wrote Charlie. 'And two suppers to follow, Mrs P.?'

'Two suppers, Charlie – and two seats by the fire for the night.' She turned to her guests.

'Nothing but chairs remaining.'

Charlie finished his writing and looked up.

'Names? What names, please?'

'Mansfield,' said the magistrate somewhat coolly – for he was more than surprised by the above formalities. 'Mr Mansfield. Justice of the Peace, sir.'

'A magistrate! Fancy that, Mrs P. Well, well, sir, it seems we're in the same line of business. For I'm a constable – among other things. Yes, sir! Here to keep law and order! And let me tell you, sir, there's not a vagabond, rogue or foot-pad who dares to set foot across the fence.'

'That's right!' agreed Mrs P. 'This cottage and all the ground enclosed by the fence belongs to the parish – and we keep it clean and above board. The law's respected here, sir.'

'And everything's recorded,' went on Charlie, patting the ledger. 'Accounts square and trim. Two measures of brandy offered; two measures of brandy writ down; two measures of brandy back from the parish. Not a drop more – not a drop less.'

'A name for honesty,' said Mrs P.

'And for neatness,' added Charlie.

Smith looked at Mr Mansfield and observed his face had grown redder than the fire could have made it. For the magistrate felt that this demonstration of upholding the law struck too shrewdly to be smiled at. And he wondered if the Parkins' neat cottage and clean garden over which they watched so exactly – and let the rest of the Common go hang – was not an image of what his own heart had been and, indeed, of the whole tidy business of the law itself.

Charlie had been about to put the ledger away, when a thought struck him.

'Lad's name, sir? Servant of your'n?'

'Friend!' said Mr Mansfield, vigorously. 'A friend!'

'Name?' said Charlie, his pen poised like a sword.

'Jones,' lied Mr Mansfield blandly.

Smith, the escaped and no doubt hunted gaol-bird, regarded the perjured magistrate with the warmest affection – and surprise.

'Jones,' wrote down Charlie, sanded the ink and shut the ledger. He looked to Mrs P.

'Shall we show why we got no bed to spare, Mrs. P.?'

'Parish business, Charlie. You ain't got the right.'

'But he's a Justice, Mrs P., and concerned, I fancy.'

'You're a sentimental vessel, Charlie Parkin. Dangerous for one with your responsibilities.'

'Just this once, Mrs P. And he's blind.'

'Very well, Charlie – as he's blind, then.'

Whereupon the sentimental constable chuckled and reopened the ledger which he carried to Mr Mansfield's side.

'There was someone before you, sir.'

'Indeed?'

'We took him in.'

'Generous, sir. Generous!'

'He was bleeding.'

'Who was he?'

'Your coachman, sir. Yes, indeed – we've succoured him and nourished him and put him to bed.'

'Thank God! Thank God!' cried Mr Mansfield, deeply moved.

'Here it is,' went on Charlie, proud to have been of service to humanity, the parish *and* a Justice of the Peace. And, forthwith, he read out the coachman's name, wound, where sustained, quantity of bandage applied, sustenance consumed and quality of lodging, together with the care of horses and use of coach-house. All of which was chargeable to the parish . . . as was the meagre warmth from Charlie Parkin's respectable heart.

Then the ledger was put away and Mrs P. busied herself with fetching hot suppers for her guests while her husband talked and talked of how he kept his garden clear and expressed the hope that Mr Mansfield would bring his vigilance to the ears of all his legal friends in Town.

At about ten o'clock the Parkins went to bed (after assuring Mr Mansfield that his coachman was not badly hurt and was sleeping peacefully) and left their guests to doze and brood in their chairs beside the banked-up fire.

'It's been a long day,' murmured Mr Mansfield.

'A long day,' agreed Smith.

'A lifetime long.'

Smith said nothing, but fancied he understood. Slowly, Mr Mansfield's head sank down on his chest and his fine, strong face glowed in the fire-light. Smith stared at him profoundly. Dreamily, he wondered what sort of man the magistrate had been before he'd lost his sight.

'Smith!'

Mr Mansfield was still awake. He'd taken off his spectacles and was staring to where he supposed Smith to be. His eyes were in a tragically ruinous state. But he was smiling. He fumbled inside his waistcoat.

'Here, Smith. Isn't this something you wanted? Take it then. Read it. Aloud, I beg of you!'

He was offering Smith the document.

Chapter 17

The document! All the time in the snow, when he and Mr Mansfield had been alone, the precious item had been within his grasp – and he'd forgotten it! Forgotten it so entirely, that its sudden appearance before the cottage fire was almost terrifying.

'Take it, Smith – and tell me what old Mr Field had to say.'

Fearfully, Smith reached out his hand and took the document. Ten thousand thoughts, fears and questions filled his head. Why had he been given it now? Why the enormous trust? Didn't the magistrate still believe him to be a murderer? But what other choice had he – in his condition? Trust was obligatory: a necessary quality of life.

'Read, Smith. Don't be afraid. Read!'

So Smith crouched down at the blind man's feet, close by the fire where the light was sufficient. And, as he sat, Mr Mansfield's hand dropped by chance on his shoulder, then moved lightly upward and rested on his head.

Smith read: slowly, shakily – for he was not over proficient and the writing was crabbed and there were words he could not pronounce.

Neither confession, nor deed to property was the document. It was a letter to Mr Lennard. A strange letter of uncanny power in the firelit room. For, as Smith read on, murdered old Mr Field seemed to creep into the parlour and cast his cold shadow between the blind man and the boy . . . so that Mr Mansfield shivered and withdrew his hand from Smith's head – and Smith shrank back towards his own side of the fire.

The old man had written in deep agitation. Something had disturbed and shaken him profoundly. Also, there was fear . . . of a distressing kind. He knew his life to be threatened. Several times, he mentioned it. 'I lie awake of nights, Lennard – and hear such sounds, and have such thoughts . . . at my age!' Then, later, he wrote of a discovery he'd made – but did not say what . . . only that he meant to carry it to his grave. A terrible discovery. This, also, was repeated and underlined . . . 'A *terrible, terrible* discovery.'

But now came an oddity. An instruction quite plain and without any of the confused fears that invaded the rest of the document. 'The trifle' (trifle was underlined) 'I wrote you of previously is buried in a shrewd place. Andrews knows where. Ask him where Jack used to play as a boy. When you have it, dispose of it as pleases you. I shall care no longer . . .' There followed some bitter and pathetic words of the world in general, all once more in a very agitated manner, together with a last reference to his discovery, reaffirming his intention of carrying it to the grave, 'where it would be hidden and forgot for ever'.

Smith stopped reading. There was a restless silence in which the fire leaped and cast strange lightnings across the blind man's face.

'Go on,' Mr Mansfield said.

'There's nothing more.'

'Nothing?'

'Nothing!' muttered Smith. 'Or d'you think I'm hiding the rest from you?'

He scowled furiously into the fire; his heart felt grievously empty. The document, the precious item that was to have raised him up in the world: nothing but an old man's misery and dread and whereabouts of a trifle – a locket, most likely, or a brooch with a twist of his grandma's hair.

For this he'd endured so much. He stared at the paper, through which the fire shone redly, and noted the stains made by his own sweat when first he'd fled from the men in brown. Then he remembered his grief when he'd thought the document had been destroyed; and then his joy when he'd discovered it was safe. He remembered Miss Fanny's hopes in it – not much less than his own . . . And now? Not even a 'whereas' or a 'felonious' or a 'property' to justify a family's dreams. Good God! And the old man had been killed for it!

'The discovery . . . the discovery,' whispered Mr Mansfield. 'What was it?'

'Took it with him to the grave,' said Smith dully. 'Dead man's wish. To be respected. Remember?'

Mr Mansfield shook his head. 'We must know it, Smith. There'll be no peace otherwise.'

'You find out on your own, Mister Mansfield. I'm done with it. I'm off.'

'But I'm blind, Smith. I – I need your eyes –'

'Your daughter's eyes are just as sharp.'

'Not so. They're partial. They're dimmed by affection. Yours, Smith, are clear.'

Smith, whose eyes were, at that time, anything but clear, being misted with tears of disappointment and general dissatisfaction with the world, nodded.

'True enough.'

Mr Mansfield frowned and his projecting brows hid his empty eyes in pools of darkness so that, to an ignorant glance, he was no more blind than the boy.

'What did you hope for from the document? Great riches? Power? What was it, Smith, that you struggled so hugely for?'

Smith did not answer, partly on account of an obscure anger against the magistrate, and partly because he'd never had a clear notion of what he'd hoped for . . . save to make his way up in the world.

Mr Mansfield waited, seeming to stare into the fire. Little by little, his head sank once more on to his chest. Smith watched him. Surely he was asleep? Maybe half an hour passed . . .

'Smith!'

'I'm here.'

'I thought you'd gone. You said you were going. Have you changed your mind?'

'I'll go in the morning.'

Once more there was silence: a long silence, broken only by the crackling of the fire and the blind man's regular breathing. Desolately, Smith stared at the unlucky document. The words jiggled and danced before his tired eyes – but never again to shape themselves into the mystery of hope.

Why had the old man been killed? As if it mattered! He was dead as mutton! Smith frowned. In the morning he'd be off, and the document, the dead man and the blind man would be left behind. Tomorrow, it would be the Town again – with all its subtle alleys and dozy pockets. Back to the beginning.

As if that were possible! Most miserably, Smith knew there could be no returning. Wherever he went, whatever he did, Curtis Court and its long consequences would haunt him. What had the old man discovered – and why had he been so coldly done in?

The blind man had been right. There'd be no peace for Smith till he knew. And, little by little, as he sat by the small fire, the desire to uncover the mystery of Mr Field's dread became as strong as his first desire to read the document itself.

No more snow had fallen in the night and now a bloodless, bewildered-looking sun stood poised on the eastern hills – as if one nudge of a cloud would topple it into snowy oblivion. Everywhere, there was an air of universal crystallization; for a frost had overlaid the snow and set tiny needles on the fatted twigs of bushes, trees and thickets, that glinted sharply, blue, green and orange.

Sometimes, these bushes took on the shapes of men, unhorsed and frozen as they'd stumbled on; here was a fellow with a slouched hat; there, one with a great nose and a pipe; and there was another, brandishing a huge pistol, fixed for the winter in a murderous aggression.

Sombrely, Smith wondered if such a fate had befallen Lord Tom and the two men in brown, for he and Mr Mansfield were on the last stage of their singular journey to Prickler's Hill and Smith was as watchful as a hawk.

He sat a-top the coach beside the wounded

coachman, who was now recovered enough – he swore – to hold the reins in his right hand; though he looked to Smith for help and support whenever the coach tipped. He'd been greatly surprised to see the 'weasel' in his master's company – and had inadvertently said so, much confusing Charlie Parkin.

'Weasel? But I understood his name was Jones. I've writ down Jones.'

'Jones? He's Smith!' declared the coachman.

'*Jones!*' said Mr Mansfield.

'Smith – Jones – Weasel . . .' muttered Charlie. 'There's more to this than meets the eye.'

'There is indeed!' agreed Mr Mansfield; and the constable never knew why the blind man laughed.

But now they were nearing the end of their journey. They skirted the village of Whetstone – and still no sign of pursuers.

'The house!' said the coachman, jerking his head towards the eminence of Prickler's Hill.

The house, built in the Palladian style, stood a third of the way up the hill, sheltered from the north by rising ground and separated from Whetstone by an old stone church whose yard, shrouded in snow, was the very image of white and peaceful sleep.

The coach could go no further. The road was steep and vilely slippery. The horses steamed and laboured in vain.

'On foot, then,' said Mr Mansfield and he bade the coachman return into Whetstone while he and Smith went forward on foot.

'Pistols, Mister Mansfield? Shall I take 'em?'

The magistrate shook his head. 'The gentlemen from Highgate Hill seem to've given up. No need for weapons now.'

Smith shrugged his shoulders, took Mr Mansfield's hand and began the last ascent. Though he could see nothing uneasy anywhere in the white landscape, he could not rid himself of the feeling that they were being watched closely. Where from? The house? The village? Or from the quiet churchyard?

He said nothing of this to Mr Mansfield, there being no sense in alarming the blind man without just cause. Instead, he listened and commented as Mr Mansfield talked of Mr Field and his unlucky life.

He learned, with but half a mind, about the disappearance and most likely death of Mr Field's only son some years before – which had been followed by so relentless a siege of the old man and his property by his brothers, their wives and children that –

'– That what, Mister Mansfield?'

'That there were suspicions – grim suspicions – that the eager family knew more than they said about the son's death.'

Smith sighed. 'D'you think that could have been the old man's discovery, Mister Mansfield? That he found out for certain what they'd done?'

Mr Mansfield had been about to answer when he felt a sudden, strong pressure from Smith's hand.

'What is it, Smith?'

'Nothing. Just the cold.'

Smith stared towards the churchyard. He was tolerably certain he'd seen something shift, slightly and secretly . . .

Chapter 18

Though Mr Field was now many weeks dead, there was still a bereaved air about his house. Dogs barked as the blind man and the boy trudged along the short, curved drive, but no one bade them be quiet – or came to see why they barked. Five yards from the door, Smith faltered.

'What is it? The cold again?'

'Freezing!' said Smith. He had fancied that he'd again seen a movement in the churchyard, which now lay below them.

The barking of the unseen dogs grew louder and to Smith it seemed they were warning, not the house, but the blind man and him to keep away – to abandon whatever it was that had brought them across the snow.

Go back! Back! Wickedness is here! The Devil is here!

But it was too late. They'd been seen approaching. The tall door opened and a footman received them. At the sound of the door the dogs fell silent and the footman nodded.

'The master's beasts, sir. There's no hushing them till they hear the door. The ignorant creatures still believe he will come back and only when they hear the door do they understand he's not come yet. For he always went to them first. Poor, ignorant beasts, God help them!'

Yet Smith felt that the footman was oddly proud of the 'ignorant beasts', and maybe thought them not so ignorant after all.

He was old, but still upright – though the worn shine of his livery across his back betrayed a straining – even a longing – to bow at last. He took Mr Mansfield's card, lowered his eyes to read it – as if to avoid the blind man's stare.

'Yes – yes, of course, sir. I should have known you. You have been before.'

'Long ago.'

'Long ago, sir.'

Now they were in the hall of Mr Field's house and Smith stared about him as if the discovery the unlucky old man had made might be written somewhere on the walls . . . or was being whispered from the faintly jingling chandelier. But the walls betrayed nothing, only some ghostly pale patches where pictures had once hung.

'Grand paintings used to be there!' said the servant with ancient pride, seeing Smith's looks.

'I remember them,' said Mr Mansfield softly. 'I remember a King Saul and David –'

'Aye, sir. That was the first to go.'

'To go?'

'Sold, sold, sir . . . to pay the butcher, the baker and –'

'– And the chimney-sweep down the road?' put in Smith quickly.

The servant looked at him curiously: then shrugged his shoulders. 'If you will, lad. The chimney-sweep down the road – whoever he may be!'

'A gent with a wooden leg.'

At this, the old servant seemed to stiffen and lose what little colour the years had left him. Then he recovered. An angry look came into his eyes, and Smith knew he'd made an enemy of the old man. But for the life of him he couldn't imagine why.

Mr Mansfield inquired for Mr Lennard but it seemed the attorney was in Barnet and would not be at the house till midday. Indeed, there was no one in the house but Miss Field (the dead master's sister) and two of the nephews.

The footman said 'no one' with a strong inflection, so that Miss Field and the nephews coming after, did indeed seem part and parcel of 'no one'. Not that the old man had been contemptuous – but there was in his voice a weariness of something too well known for contempt.

'The others are with Mr Lennard, sir. They are always with Mr Lennard. They give him no peace, sir, – not even to conduct the business. He stayed here, sir, for two nights. But he had to leave. They were at him all the while. Poor souls! For they're in need even of the necessary penny to bless themselves with . . . and so will go to hell. For who will bless them now? Not I! Not I!'

They were now come into the chief drawing-room: a long, handsome apartment with tall windows giving out on to the church and Whetstone beyond it. There was a fire in the grate, but it burned cheerlessly, with uneasy flames and little heat. Here, too, there were ghosts on the walls . . . and a small writing-table by one of the windows.

Was it here he'd written of the discovery that had sent him hurrying to the Town?

Smith stared sombrely out of the window towards the churchyard. Once more, he had the feeling of being secretly watched.

'Not I,' said the servant for a third time; and his grim sentiment was not to be answered.

'You are a hard fellow,' said Mr Mansfield sternly; for hardness begets hardness.

'I am an old man, sir, and in the course of nature, I'll soon be with my master. *Then* I'll make my reckoning with the Almighty; but before that I must finish my account with Mr Field. Though he is dead, sir, my duty to him is not.'

He assisted Mr Mansfield to a chair which the blind man, being unused to the hands that were guiding him, felt carefully and exactly. He frowned. The upholstery was much torn – a strange state of affairs in so short a time since the master's death.

But it was not that chair alone; everywhere in the room, cushions and seats were in a grievous state – with their white insides peeping forth for all the world as though the wild, pervasive snow had crept into the house and hid itself everywhere.

'Aye,' said the servant. ''Tis the same elsewhere. You'll not find a cushion, chair-covering nor bolster unslit, nor a floorboard unopened. The family have been hard at it. For they've a heathenish belief the master hid a great fortune somewhere against the chance of – of poor dead Jack's returning! But Jack will come back when his father does – and that will be at the Judgement of us all! Not a day before! Aye! And *then* the beasts will bark and bark!'

(But where did Jack play as a boy? suddenly wondered Smith – with an excitement that had been steadily mounting within him as he remembered the document's injunction.)

Now the servant – after brushing some ash from the hearth, on which the fire looked more wretched than ever – left the room to announce Mr Mansfield to Miss Field. Smith and the blind man were alone.

'Andrews!' muttered Smith urgently. 'We'd best ask Andrews where Jack played as a boy!'

'Why? D'you still have your hopes? If so – forget

them, Smith. We'll wait for Mr Lennard. This is his affair alone.'

The blind man spoke sharpishly – as if Smith had suddenly lost ground with him. He breathed deeply – and provoked a silence, in which he regretted profoundly what he'd said. But there was no other way. He was much tormented. Though he trusted Smith with his very life, he could not trust him with the dead man's secret. He dreaded the boy would be off, never to be found again in the dark world – save to be hanged.

He said, more gently, 'Where are you now?'

'By the fire.'

'Oh yes – yes . . .'

'Why did you ask?'

'I – I thought you were over there.' He pointed to the windows. 'I thought you were staring at me.'

But before Smith could answer Miss Field came hurriedly into the room. She was a gaunt-boned, elderly lady – large, though frail and anxious-looking. She rustled tremendously as she moved – like great sweepings of autumn leaves.

'Mr Mansfield! Kate Field at your service, sir!' She held out a hand – looked puzzled when it wasn't taken – then flushed at her mistake and glanced apologetically at Smith, as if she'd wounded *him*.

'Sad times, Mr Mansfield! A brother dead . . . the family penniless! Sell, sell, sell! But we must! To live, you know! I expect you've noticed great change – Oh!' Once more she flushed and bit her lip. 'But how's dear little Rose? It – it *is* Rose, isn't it, sir?'

She seemed particularly anxious to get *something* right, and was much relieved when the blind man nodded. So she went breathlessly on, shifting about the room – even picking at the ruined furnishings, like a large black moth in search of a meal.

She faintly resembled her murdered brother – and this touched Smith curiously, so that, when she returned – as she often did – to the family's distress and disappointed hopes and desperation for money, he could not share the blind man's indifference. Why shouldn't the silly old woman long for money? And be open about it? Steeped as he was in the darknesses of the Town, Smith understood too well Miss Field's painful distraction – that had pushed out even seemly grief at her brother's death.

Then abruptly, Miss Field realized she was not recommending herself to anyone but the curious urchin the magistrate had brought with him: she cast a rapid, melancholy smile at Smith and began to talk hurriedly and sadly about the dead man.

'Yes – yes . . . a sad life, my brother's! A tragedy, Mr Mansfield! Never, never for a day did he get over the loss of Jack, never accepted it. The shock, I suppose. Always expected him to come riding up the drive. Tragic! Even turned on the rest of us when we tried to tell him. Tragic for *us*! *We* only meant to help. And – believe me, it was for the best!' (Here, she glanced uneasily at the servant – as if she suspected him of something worse than contempt.) 'Not a worthy son! Not likeable. Though I was his aunt, I say it – and God forgive me – he's better off dead! But – but we mustn't speak ill of them – the dead, I mean – for there they lie –' (She was by the window, momentarily looking out.) '– in the churchyard: my brother and his dear wife . . . Well, well! Maybe he's with his precious Jack in heaven now.' (She glanced almost defiantly at the servant, who turned away.) 'And maybe he repents of having hid his fortune away from us! Cruel, cruel thing to do! Unnatural, don't you think, Mr Mansfield?'

Mr Mansfield's lips were tight – and Smith was sorry for it. He was, at that time, sorry for a great many things: not least that the long search and deep pursuit should end in this cheerless, ransacked house with the pitiful old lady somehow driving a deeper wedge than ever between him and the implacable blind man.

'*Our* tragedy, Mr Mansfield! It's all *our* tragedy! Everyone turns against us! Even Attorney Lennard. Oh, I can tell! He turns away – he frowns – he would not stay here. *God knows* what he thinks of us all! You come at a sad time, sir! And all on account of the money! Oh, where can it be? *God knows* we've done our part! *God knows* we've searched!' (She stared at the torn furnishings.) 'Oh, it's cruel! And yet it *must* be somewhere – Ah!'

She stopped as a far-off tumbling was heard. 'My nephews in the attic, sir. I must go! Pray to God they've found something! Pray to *God*!'

She was already half through the door – when she remembered her responsibilities. 'Do forgive me, sir. Mind on other things. Our tragedy, you know. Serve wine, Andrews!'

With that, she was gone, leaving Smith to stare, dismayed, at the old servant of whom he'd made an enemy. At Andrews, who held the key to one secret at least.

'Ask him!' breathed Smith desperately into the blind man's ear as Andrews was at a side-table. But the magistrate grimly shook his head.

Back came Andrews with a glass of wine for Mr

Mansfield – and for Smith, a deeply hostile look. So Smith returned to staring restlessly and unhappily through the windows. An obscure feeling of haste was gripping him . . . as if he'd been infected by the general unquiet of the house itself. Outside, the churchyard was hid by snow-hatted yews. But up stood the bell tower on tiptoe – with an air of stony peeping.

Andrews was talking with Mr Mansfield about Jack. Defending the dead son against the unjust attack. Andrews was very jealous of the dead's good name: both father and son. For the living, he'd not so much to say. And the blind man was nodding gravely as he heard how well and handsomely Jack had grown to manhood – instead of asking Andrews where Jack had played as a boy. 'Dead man's wishes!' Smith longed to cry out. 'To be respected! Ask of Andrews where Jack used to play as a boy!'

'It's twelve years now,' went on Andrews. 'And still they've not forgiven him for being loved! Still they dislike him – abuse him – hate and envy him – as if he will indeed come riding up the drive and snatch some trifle out of their greedy hands!'

'Is it twelve years already, Andrews?'

Twelve years it was, and Jack had been just

twenty – with the world before him. And then – he'd vanished. Gone into London it was supposed, and been swallowed up. There was a tale he'd been pressed aboard a ship that had gone down with all hands off the Lizard. But did it matter now? After twelve years the dead lie deep and it's only their good name that can be distressed.

'So why can't they let him rest in peace with his father?' Andrews nodded to the windows and beyond, and the peering belfry seemed to nod back. Yet the yews had a secret air . . . These yews were not so close together as Smith had at first supposed. Here and there were thin gaps. Was it from these gaps that came the sense of watching?

'I'll leave you now, sir,' Andrews was saying, and Smith's desperation grew extreme. He sensed that Mr Mansfield was lost to him. All that remained was 'the trifle'. Such hopes as he had, had dwindled to that, and he clung to them as if for his life. It was eleven o'clock. The attorney was to come at midday. Smith believed he'd an hour remaining. (But the time was shorter than he dreamed.)

'Mister Andrews!' he cried out.

The servant's hand was on the door. He paused.

'Tell us – what was Jack like as – as a boy?'

'Smith!' muttered the magistrate unhappily.

But Andrews – for some reason – turned to answer.

'Why – he was well-built . . . very well-built. Handsome. Oh yes! And thoughtful. He was of a thoughtful disposition.'

'Were he like me, then?'

'He was – country bred.' (With a sneer.)

'D'you mean he didn't run an' climb an' play like – like other lads?' went on Smith – who'd done none of these things, save run. 'Didn't he 'ave no favourite places to nip into when the going was 'ot? Didn't he 'ave no little alley or court he could call his own, Mister Andrews?'

'Smith!' whispered the blind man fiercely.

'For if he didn't, Mister Andrews, he weren't a very natural boy!'

Andrews – touched on a raw place – answered almost contemptuously: 'Where you, boy, might make a nest in a dirty corner of the wicked Town, Jack, when the secret mood was on him (such as comes to all boys who love to dream), would go –'

'– Where? Where would he go?'

Smith's excitement was intense. So near – so near!

'Smith –'

But Andrews had already crossed the room. Not even the furious magistrate could prevent him defending the dead Jack's quality against the urchin.

With wide eyes Smith watched him. He halted by the window. He pointed – and Smith's blood chilled!

'*There* was Jack's nest! In yonder churchyard – by the statue of a carved black angel. *There* he'd sit and dream his dreams – and, maybe, even watch us all –'

Andrews was gone from the room. Mr Mansfield had heard him take his leave.

'Smith!' he whispered, urgently. No answer. 'Smith! Smith! Where are you?'

Silence and darkness . . . deeper than the blind man had ever known it. The boy was gone!

He rose to his feet and began, with desperate haste, to feel his way towards the last sound he'd heard: the door closing. The empty air mocked at him – offering the feeling of obstacles, then declaring: Nothing here, blind man – as he jerked and staggered until, thankfully, he struck against the wall.

'Smith! Smith! Come back! You're mad, child! You'll damn yourself. No one will help you now, Smith!'

He found the door, opened it, and felt cold air

blowing in his face. This he knew he must follow. He prayed to God no one would see him as he tottered foolishly, ridiculously, after the urchin to whom he seemed uncannily chained.

'Smith ... Smith!' he kept whispering into what he imagined were corners, in the hope the child was hiding from him – was playing a cruel game – was only pretending to be gone to the damnable churchyard to dig up 'the trifle', to be gone for ever into the implacable silence and dark. 'Voices in the night' he'd said on a certain terrible day. Did he know the truth of it? And did he know what the dark was like when the voices were gone? Did he know the *other* voices that plague a blind man?

'Smith – Smith –'

He was now very near the source of the cold air. He heard a chandelier jingling as a draught stirred it. He was in the hall. The front door was open.

'Smith!' he called helplessly and fell out into the snow. Much shaken, he struggled upright.

'Smith!' he cried out, as loudly as he dared, for he was committed too deeply with the invisible, infant criminal to court any other's knowledge of it. He'd perjured himself for him; he'd given up a dead man's trust to him; he'd broken the law and compromised his own honour for him; he'd wracked himself for him – and because of what? Wretchedly, he shook his head – and the snow fell away from his hair. 'Child! Come back to me! Smith – I'm frightened . . . for you . . . for me! Smith –'

There was no answer – nothing but the restless motion of cold air through unseen shrubs. And then a dog began to bark, then another, and another! A shrill, dreadful sound in the blind man's ears. For the creatures now sounded ferocious, as if warning of a new crisis in the house's affairs which they – if they were loosed – could avert. Was it him they would tear and snap at? Or was there someone else on his way?

Suddenly, a hand clutched at his wrist and dragged him furiously to one side. Smith had come back.

'Smith –'

'Quiet! Someone's on his way! The ignorant beasts have gone mad again!'

Smith's voice was low and trembling. He sounded frightened half to death. Had he already been to the churchyard?

'Child –'

'Quiet, I tell you!' His grip on the blind man's wrist was almost vicious in its strength – as if the boy were exacting such small vengeance as he could for having been drawn back. But Smith had conceived with dread that the dogs were barking the approach of the two men in brown!

He'd seen the blind man swaying in the drive. He'd heard him calling. But he had not moved till the dogs barked. So where had he been, so still and quiet and unbreathing, even? By the lych-gate of the churchyard . . . staring into the snow. Certain footprints had appalled him, frozen him body and soul – till he'd heard the warning dogs; which sound had awoken him.

'Where are you dragging me, child?'

'To the churchyard.'

'Why?'

'You'll see.'

'Have you forgotten – I'm blind?'

'Not that blind, Mister Mansfield.'

The dogs were still barking. Whoever was coming was not yet near enough to disappoint them. Smith fancied he heard a carriage door . . . but still he dragged Mr Mansfield through the concealing bushes, enjoining him to absolute quiet; there was yet more to fear than whatever the dogs barked at and yet more to discover than ever those creatures would learn.

Down, down to the churchyard – with the snow flurrying secretly about them – hurried the boy and the blind man, till they were at the lych-gate. The blind man felt the boy halt a moment: he felt his fingers tremble and grip tighter than ever before; he heard him draw in his breath. Then they went inside . . .

Still and silent was the little garden where the dead were planted and bloomed in stone. Very prettily did the headstones wear their widows' caps of snow and stand respectfully in groups and rows.

But even in death there's ambition, and a carved black angel knelt upon one tomb as if to say: What a special one lies here.

Now this angel knelt upon a flat stone to which mounted three steps. Upon these steps was a second figure, still enough to be likewise carved. A figure with an easy, familiar air – as if he was come back at last to a place much loved in childhood – the figure of a man with a wooden leg . . .

Chapter 19

Still knowing nothing for certain but the need for extreme secrecy, the blind man suffered himself to be pulled and dragged down till he felt the stone of the church at his back and heard Smith's voice breathe close in his ear: 'He's there, by the statue! Peg-top! Old Hop-an'-Scrape! Whispering Jack! Jack o' the alley! Little Jackie Field – and the spitting image of his done-for Pa! It's my *Mister Black*!'

'The son! Alive?'

'Yes. More's the pity! It was him what done

the old man in. Little, limping, whispering Jack!'

'Horrible, horrible!'

'He's not of your opinion! For he's a-smiling, there. He's of a thoughtful disposition, he is. Country bred. Who'd have thought the Devil was born among the green fields out Barnet way? Yes – he's a-smiling very thoughtful. You got no eyes, friend, and you should be thankful. For you ain't missing much!'

So now they knew – beyond all doubt – what discovery the old man had made and sought to take with him to the grave. He had discovered his son was still alive – and would have been better dead. That the hope, the dream, the golden place in his life was as wicked and monstrous a morsel of man and wood as stalked and whispered and hid anywhere in the world.

To this dreadful thing, the document had at last led Smith and Mr Mansfield . . . to this one-legged gentleman, squatting in the shadow of a carved angel's wing, smiling broodily, with the air of having come by appointment . . . Fearfully, Smith's mind went back to his one-time hopes that the document would raise him up in the world. Instead, it had given him a sight of depths past even his darkest dreams.

But the one-legged gentleman was looking up. Someone was coming – keeping the appointment. Who'd arranged to meet with the Devil?

'Here he comes!' breathed Smith, with bitter triumph. 'Yore friend and mine.'

For into the churchyard, skipping across the snow with his black coat-tails flapping – like a prosperous bird of prey – came the neat Mr Billing!

'Jack!' he called gently.

'Billing!'

Mr Mansfield stiffened as if to rise. Grimly, Smith held him back. He would have the magistrate hear all there was to be heard.

'The document. Have you got it?' This, from Mr Billing who was come to 'Mr Black's' side.

'No. Our brown friends are not yet come.'

'Ah well, it won't be long now, dear Jack!' Mr Billing laid his hand round the other's shoulder. The one-legged man seemed to shiver slightly – as if submitting with an ill-grace.

'As you say – not long, dear Billing . . . and we'll be rid of each other!'

'Why, Jack! We're friends! Have been so for years. Why the bitterness – now?'

'You made me kill him, Billing.'

'*I* made you? Jack, Jack, it's not so.'

'*You* planned! *You* urged! *You* tempted!'

'Ah, but *you* acted, Jack! Never forget that!'

'How can I? Not till I die. And, maybe, not even then.' He looked up at the black angel – then back to the attorney with a harsh groan. 'And d'you remember, you even swore it would be Andrews coming –'

'A murder's a murder, Jack – no matter who perishes. But don't blame yourself, dear. It's not you – or me. It's this world we live in, Jack! What can we do? We've got to live. Take the rough with the smooth, Jack. It'll all come out in the wash! If there's a God in heaven – He knows the difficulties we're up against down here. He'll understand. He'll forgive us. And – if there's no such Judge – well, Jack, what have we got to lose? It's all in the mind, my dear! Well, well – we'd all like to be saints through and through. Nothing nicer. But we can't. It's the world, Jack, not us. And we can't change that. No, sir!'

In the quiet, cold air, the voices carried intimately, so's no inflection, even, was lost on the listeners. It was not Mr Black, then, but Mr Billing who was the Devil! Mr Black was but the outward image of evil – its eyes, teeth, hands, skin and hair – but Mr Billing was its inward, horrible, cajoling, obliging soul!

They continued murmuring, in a like vein, for a while longer, and it became plain it was not for the first time. There was a weariness in Mr Black's bitterness and a boredom in the attorney's evasions that bespoke much repetition. Over and above them, the black angel brooded thoughtfully . . . and somewhere beneath them lay whatever it was they'd murdered for: the buried trifle.

But now, a slight breeze sprang up, lifting little tufts of snow from the stones, as if there were a restlessness below – a stirring . . .

'Oh God for Judgement!' groaned Mr Mansfield. 'But what sort of Judgement can there be?'

'At last!' exclaimed the terrible Mr Black. 'They've come!'

And the yet more terrible Mr Billing smiled and waved.

From the far end of the churchyard, through the quiet yews, came the two men in brown. Very dark-faced and frozen they were, as they approached their employers. But the breeze quickened, and their exchanges were partly lost.

'. . . the document?'

'. . . not got it!'

'. . . not? Why not? Not killed the blind man, then?'

They shook their wicked heads. Mr Black – grey with terror and rage – raised his hand to strike at them. But Mr Billing – everyone's friend – stayed his hand, and did not free it. Instead, he forced it down . . . and made it point – (Would Mr Billing have used even his own finger? Not if another was to hand!) – to the snow. What was so remarkable about the snow? Footmarks. There were his own. There – so curious that they'd chilled Smith's blood when he'd first spied them – were the one-legged man's. And . . . two sets more – not to be accounted for – leading through the gate.

Through the gate, close by the church wall, to a certain old tree.

'They've found us!' whispered Smith. 'We ain't got a chance, Mister Mansfield. Judgement's come all right – but it's come for us!'

Slowly, the two men in brown turned to peer at the tree. Then a single grin spread over their faces. They began to walk.

The breeze grew into a wind and the snow about their feet shuddered and shifted as if there was a creeping turmoil below.

'Kill them!' screamed Mr Billing abruptly. 'No help for it! You've got to do it!'

Could Smith have escaped? In all certainty, yes!

He'd the agility, the quickness, the wit and the terror to vanish from the abominable churchyard before the men had covered half the distance. But not so Mr Mansfield. The old 'mole-in-the-hole' could never have got further than the gate without a sharp knife in his broad back. So Smith, with all his quickness, wit and terror, lacked the last ingredient for flight: the will. He was not capable of leaving the blind man behind.

'They're a-coming, Mister Mansfield.'

'Then for God's sake, go!'

'For God's sake! That's a queer thing!'

The men were now very close. They carried short, glittering knives. Already they could see Smith and were grinning widely – even encouragingly – at him.

Now Smith, in spite of all his knowledge of the worst of the Town – its rogues and vagrants, its thieves and slinking by-ways – was really no more than a child . . . and he turned to childish weapons for his last defence. With small, trembling fingers he made a snowball, stood up and, with a loud, defiant shriek, flung it at the nearer of the advancing pair.

The man swore – but stopped. His companion – instead of dispatching the boy – laughed. A very costly laugh, that. The seconds thus spent were important.

Momentarily, the wind puffed up a little storm of snow and out of it – as if resurrected from under the white ground itself – staggered a formidable figure.

'Stop! Hold! Stand, there!'

Cloaked, large, pistolled, stood Lord Tom!

'You dirty great bag of wind! Be off with you!' snarled the man with snow in his face.

'Spare the boy! I'll – I'll not have him harmed!'

'*You'll* not? And who's *you*, Lord piddling Tom? Be off – or we'll slit you in tiny pieces, friend!'

Lord Tom's frostily bristling face grew pitifully angry.

'Smut!' he called, waving vaguely. 'Never fear! Lord Tom's beside you! I'll save you, lad! I'll blow blue daylight through 'em!'

'Be off, Lord Tom!' answered Smith bitterly. 'You'd best save your own lousy skin. I'm done with you now! I know you, Lord Tom. And I don't like what I know!'

The huge highwayman flinched. He screwed up his little eyes. Whether or not he really loved the boy was hard to say. Maybe he did, maybe the sharp wound he'd just received was all but mortal.

And so, maybe from this moment on, he was fighting for more than his life; he was fighting for his soul.

'Back! Back!' shouted Lord Tom, with the utmost valour and rage.

'And if we don't?' sneered the two men.

'Then you're dead as mutton!'

For a second time, the smaller of the two men in brown laughed. He steadied his knife. Took a pace forward –

'Blue daylight!' roared Lord Tom and fired.

A terrible, double roar; a terrible, double shout and the man who laughed – laughed no more. He was dead. And Lord Tom – Lord Tom, much astonished – was capering foolishly in the snow, opening and shutting his mouth in defiant shouts that emerged as silent puffs of scarlet air.

There was a ball inside of him. Mr Black had shot him even as he'd discharged his own pistol. Lord Tom was as good as dead, but he seemed not to know it yet. Instead, with the meagre remains of his life, he threatened the second of the two men with a pistol that was suddenly grown marvellously heavy. And this second fellow, seeing his companion dead, waited no longer. Wildly, he rushed away.

Lord Tom's dance grew slower and comically clumsy as he strove to lift his great boots out of the clinging snow. Even as the amazed and suddenly heart-broken Smith watched, all the fire and fury and daring rage drained out of his old hero's face. He halted, tottering, then sank upon his knees, curiously crossing his pistols upon his chest, where there was a warm, gushing pain.

'Ha – ha! Blue daylight, eh, lad?'

They were alone in the graveyard now. Mr Black had hopped crazily in the wake of his adviser and friend Mr Billing. They'd heard sounds from the house and escaped. The shots had set up an alarm. The dogs were howling wretchedly.

Lord Tom lay with his head on the lowest of the steps where Mr Black had sat and waited. Above him brooded the stone angel. If he knew he was done for, the sight must have frightened him. Yet he showed none of it. Sadly, Smith approached him, leading blind Mr Mansfield.

'Glad to make your – acquaintance, sir! Never – never thought to! Ha-ha! Shake hands? Really, an honour –'

'And for me, Lord Tom. And for me!'

Solemnly, their hands, guided by Smith, met and grasped: the dying highwayman's and the blind magistrate's. And both were glad of it, for both had reached the end of a journey: for Lord Tom it was the last, but for Mr Mansfield it was, maybe, his first. A very strange journey – from justice to compassion.

Now Lord Tom closed his eyes and from out of his side a red patch blossomed in the snow, spread and gently melted into tiny scarlet needles and caves . . . then filled up.

'Nights on the Common, Smut!' he whispered. 'Duval . . . Turpin . . . Robinson . . . and – and –'

'– And Lord Tom!' wept Smith, for his friend was dead.

And so was Mr Black. Andrews had followed him, as he leapt and hopped away. He'd taken a fowling-piece, caught him this side of Whetstone, and shot him dead.

Mr Black lay like a malformed dark star in the snow – a giant child's star, with a wooden stick to hold it by – that shadowy, formidable ruin of a good man's son.

What had been his history? As dark and shadowy as the rest of him. Where had he lived, how lost his leg, how met with his corrupt adviser? These were questions to which there were no answers. All that was known for certain was that he'd fled his home twelve years before and never dared return on account of some hanging offence. This, Andrews knew of, and preferred that the world and Mr Field should think Jack dead rather than damned. A heavy secret – and the granity old fellow's shoulders were bending under it.

But to hide an evil is not to destroy it. The old man had made his discovery and had been hurried into his grave.

Andrews must have stood a great while upon a hillock above the fallen figure for, when Mr Lennard's coach came towards Prickler's Hill, he was still there, looking to the sky, as if the spread shape below had fallen a great way to this cold, white ruin.

But of Mr Billing there was no sign, and it seemed for a while as though the earth itself had swallowed him up. No one saw him – neither anyone in the house, nor Mr Lennard coming from Barnet, nor Miss Mansfield coming a-foot from Whetstone, where Mr Billing, whom she'd insisted on accompanying, had begged her to remain, as if to spare her from the tragic news he was confident was awaiting – that her father had been murdered on Finchley Common. There was no doubt that this vile and hateful man still loved Miss Mansfield; for the sake of which spark of humanity in him, maybe his sentence in the courts of heaven will be to burn in hell for one day less than if he'd never loved at all.

Chapter 20

Mournful Smith, Smith of disasters, Smith who'd led the blind so fatefully – storm-tossed, heartbroken Smith. He stared through the windows of the house to the widowy yew trees behind which lay his idol, Lord Tom.

His snow-stained, tear-stained face came but rarely out of its faraway look to survey the busy drawing-room and only the most serious commotion could hold him for long. The coming of Mr Lennard, together with as many of the old man's family as could get into his coach, interested him but little; and even Mr Mansfield's proud introduction of him to the old-fashioned lawyer with his old-fashioned face – 'My guardian angel, sir! A little singed and tattered about the wings – but then he's flown through the caves of hell! Meet Smith.' – even this grand introduction provoked but a melancholy smile.

'Pleased to meet you,' he muttered, 'I'm sure,' and turned back to the viewing of his private grief.

Lord Tom – Lord Tom! You blew blue daylight through 'em just like you said! Oh, Lord Tom – you went like the grandest toby of them all!

Cowardice, boastfulness and double-dealing had bled out of Lord Tom into the snow and what remained in Smith's heart was 'the grandest toby of them all'.

Then Miss Mansfield came and Smith turned and smiled compassionately across the room at her. She'd learned of Mr Billing's monstrousness and the pain and bitterness in her heart was written in her eyes. Quickly, she crossed to the window, put her arm about Smith's shoulder and pressed her cold face to his, so that her dark hair curtained them off in a private night.

'Sorry you lost a friend, miss,' he said. Then he

turned away even from her, to the dark yew trees and the strangely moving whiteness beyond.

'Smith,' murmured Mr Mansfield, who had not left his side. 'What did he – look like?'

Smith sniffed and swallowed hard. ''E was a big man, Mister Mansfield, and always wore green. Green 'at, green cloak, green breeches – and 'e'd bright green eyes as well. 'E bristled a bit about the chops, but 'ad such a smile on 'im when he talked of the Common, that 'e fair shone. 'E was a real gallant 'igh toby, Mister Mansfield. One of the best!'

'He – went well, Smith.'

'None better, Mister Mansfield.'

'He's in heaven, Smith.'

'If there's Commons up there, that's where 'e is, Mister Mansfield. Right up 'igh on the snaffling lay!'

Then Mr Lennard came over, followed by the inquisitive eyes of Mr Field's family – the beneficiaries of nothing in particular. He began to talk in low tones to Mr Mansfield and Smith's mournful attention drifted away; till a piece of sardonic humour struck him – a wry, Smith-like humour.

Mr Mansfield was mentioning his name and handing over the document to Mr Lennard. With an awful smile Smith watched the stained and tattered paper change hands. In a moment, it was done.

'Bleeding mail-boy, that's what I been!' he brooded. 'Documents took and delivered. No charge. And you may 'ave confidence. I'll rent me an office in the shadow of St Paul's. Come wind, come snow, come Newgate Gaol and the deaths of friends – Smith gets through with the documents! From Curtis Court to Prickler's Hill in less than three months! Well done, Smith!'

But Mr Lennard had come now to 'the trifle'. Mild interest tickled Smith – in spite of his aching heart. It was proposed to go at once to the burying place. Smith sighed. He'd no wish to visit that spot so soon, but the beneficiaries were eager.

'Come, Smith,' murmured Mr Mansfield, hearing sounds of movement to the door. 'Let's see it out.'

So Smith, still heavy of heart, but nonetheless inquisitive enough not to be left behind, followed the respectfully hopeful beneficiaries to the sheeted churchyard. Strange occasion: strange procession; to go to a churchyard in hope.

Through the well-remembered little gate they wound, past the rents in the snow to show where the dead man in brown and the mortality of Lord Tom had been decently dragged away.

'He's gone,' whispered Smith, and Mr Mansfield took off his hat.

Black and peaceful was the angel, undisturbed at its mysterious devotions though the world had rocked and tumbled about it.

'Is this the place?'

Andrews nodded. This was the place.

The sexton was fetched from the church and, under a host of desperate eyes, he began to dig.

Strangely like the old man himself were the crowding beneficiaries, thought Smith, as he watched them moving their lips in silent prayer. Like echoes of him: there was his nose, there his chin and there, in his frail, gaunt sister, were his very eyes. Indeed, it was as though Mr Field was come back to see his wishes at last fulfilled.

Smith turned to watch the toiling sexton who'd pierced the snow and was a foot into the frozen earth. He paused to wipe his brow. Hard on the beneficiaries – to wait while he drew breath. He grunted and continued.

'Ah! What 'ave we 'ere?'

A straining forward: an excitement.

'No. Nothing. A slab of stone. Sorry, good people.'

A general perishing of excitement. A gloom,

almost. Old Miss Field had begun to weep. Smith bowed his small, storm-tossed head. Was everyone to be disappointed?

'Ah! What 'ave we 'ere?'

The sexton was looking up, frowning. What had been buried and not by him? A trifle. A wooden box . . . a travelling box . . .

'It was *his*!' whispered Miss Field. 'I know it! He always used to take it with him to –'

'But 'e's left it behind now, ma'am!' grunted the sexton and struck off the strap with his spade.

It may be that it's unseemly for beneficiaries to beam and twinkle in a churchyard – even to caper gently in the snow and crowd and shake a lawyer's hand. But in God's name, what else were they to do? Crocodiles might have wept, but the beneficiaries were needy human souls.

Mr Field's wooden box was filled, stuffed and glutted with a prosperous lifetime's guineas! Guineas that lay upon guineas in sunny shoals, gleaming and winking in the cold light. The old man must have carried them there in bags which had long since split and sunk under the spreading weight of coinage for, here and there, tufts of canvas poked up, like threads of cloud in a golden sky.

A hundred thousand! thought Smith dreamily. Must be a hundred thousand golden flatties down there! God save the King! For Smith, whenever he saw a sight too grand for any of his words, always said, 'God save the King!'

And sometime later that morning, when the company – in radiant spirits – were back in the house, he had occasion to say once more, 'God save the King!'

It is night in the Red Lion Tavern between Turnmill Street and Saffron Hill. In the cellar, Miss Fanny and Miss Bridget – reduced to four or five smoking tallows – are sewing mournfully. Miss Fanny has heard of the death of her admirer and is red-eyed and sniffy. Miss Bridget does not speak but sighs and shrugs her shoulders from time to time. Their shadows hugely comment on them upon the wall.

Miss Bridget looks up as if she will speak – but thinks better of it and returns to her work. Miss Fanny loudly sniffs again.

Suddenly, there are certain sounds from above. Miss Bridget frowns and shakes her head. (Her great shadow does likewise, as if in agreement.) But Miss Fanny puts down her work with an air of presentiment.

'It's him!'

'Never!'

'It's him, Brid! It's him!'

The door opens. There's a clatter and scuffle. Once more, Smith has missed his footing and fallen down the stairs!

'It's him! It's Smut!' cries Miss Fanny, dropping her work entirely and bustling to her feet.

'And about time, too!' says Miss Bridget, looking as stern as she might. 'Oh, you felonious child! We thought you was shamefully dead!'

Now Smith picks himself up, rubs his elbows, the side of his head and a shin. He squints disparagingly round the cellar, then grandly at his sisters.

'Dead?' he says. 'What business would I 'ave being dead with ten thousand guineas to me name? Answer me that!'

And he stares at them with such an air of offended dignity and unnatural honesty, that they're half inclined to believe him. The half so inclined is Miss Fanny. The half which is not, is Miss Bridget – who's worked hard all of her young life and never dreamed of being related to more than twenty pound in cash.

Resolutely, she's ever set her handsome but

toil-sterned face against her softer sister's imaginings, saying over and over again that such gaudy thoughts are as tinsel thread – fit enough to decorate a bodice, but never to hold up a hem. Tears start to her eyes as she sees her sister dote and smile foolishly upon the small Smith whose heart she thought she knew as being closer to her own.

Of a sudden, Miss Bridget feels tired and lonely in the seedy world of the Red Lion's cellar. Why must it always be me, she thinks, who's got to spoil the dreaming? Do they suppose I like this shameful place? But someone must face it out – for we can't live off dreams alone!

'What would you say,' says Smith, adding insult to injury by disengaging himself from Miss Fanny and coming to outface the stern Miss Bridget herself, 'to a carriage an' pair, and a 'ouse in Golden Square?'

Miss Bridget looks at her silly sister and the thin child whose sharp face is fairly shining with pleasure. She sighs. Why not? she thinks. What harm in a few hours of cheerful dreaming? Soon enough the grey, grey dawn. So Miss Bridget nods and smiles and reaches out to ruffle Smith's head.

'I'd say, child, I'd like it very much. When do we move?'

'Tomorrow,' says Smith. 'And what would you say to a footman, a maid and a coachie?'

'I'd say, very elegant, child. When do we engage them?' Is it possible Miss Bridget is beginning to enjoy the dreaming – or are her eyes shining only because she's warmed by Smith's generosity even in his dreams?

'Tomorrow,' says Smith.

'Oh, Smut!' cries Miss Fanny. 'You are good! Might we have a tall coachman, in green livery?'

Smith nods in an off-hand fashion. 'And what would you say to offering me old friend Mister Magistrate Mansfield of Vine Street a tot of what might warm him against the cold night air?'

Miss Bridget smiles. 'I'd say it would be an honour and we'd be very pleased to oblige. When do we invite him?'

'Now!' says Smith and shouts: 'Come in, Mister Mansfield! I prepared 'em! Mind the steps. There's thirteen!'

Upon which Miss Fanny shrieks and Miss Bridget goes white as her stockings, for the door has opened and the great blind magistrate himself stands incredibly at the head of the stairs.

'Good evening, ladies. I've heard much about you –'

Very pitiable to behold is now Miss Bridget, for she's gone quite distracted and begins to fly about the cellar in a terrible frenzy of tidying and making seemly. Her thoughts are in a whirl and she knows not if she's on her head or her heels. She keeps crying out very breathlessly: 'Oh, Smut! You should have said – you should have warned – Oh, Smut!'

Till Smith puts an end to her cellar-proud misery by saying: 'Don't fret, Miss Bridget. He's as blind as a mole. If it wasn't for the whiff, he might as well be in St James's Palace! Ain't that so, Mister Mansfield?'

And the great man smiles and nods and Miss Bridget is no longer in any doubt of which way up she is: she *knows* she is on her head!

And that was how Smith came home: Smith of the courts and alleys: Smith of the corners and byways and many a passing pocket: Smith the ten thousand guinea man! For he'd spoke not a halfpenny less than the truth.

On the morning at Prickler's Hill – to the beneficiaries' approval and his own speechless (save for 'God save the King!') delight, Attorney Lennard had awarded him one tenth of the churchyard treasure as a mark of gratitude and esteem: ten thousand guineas!

'A good, round sum,' had said Mr Mansfield, with satisfaction. 'And what are you going to do with it, Smith?' But Smith has answered never a word, for he'd fainted away on 'King'!

Small wonder, then, that Miss Bridget was distracted and, even after an hour with the magistrate sitting beside her talking gently and wisely of all their futures, still believed she'd fallen a victim to her sister's foolish dreaming and was no more awake than a bed-post!

But at last, when morning brought no gloomy fact to dispel the night's fancy, she permitted herself to believe that the future was a rosy and splendid affair . . . and even to tolerate, with a gracious smile, her sister's favourite remark that, 'I always said, Brid, that there was *some* good in our dockiment, didn't I?'

Though there was no more snow, the weather continued very cold until the beginning of March, when an unlooked-for warmth set in, and the sun came out in spring-like glory. Everywhere, the snow – which had grown as flat, tired and grubby as an old sheet – went into little green holes. Then, swiftly, these holes spread into islands which put out fingers, like children in a round dance, eager to touch their neighbours. So the green islands joined up and the whiteness shrank away till it vanished entirely, and nothing more was left of the snow but a crusty puddle or two in the vicinity of Godliman Street and Curtis Court, where Mr Lennard, the attorney, has his office and sometimes works late . . . for he's short of a partner. Even though, one night, Mr Billing came quietly and furtively back!

Much shocked, amazed and a trifle uneasy, Mr Lennard let him in after warning him that he must and would have him arrested for his monstrous villainy.

'Don't be too harsh on me, sir!' Mr Billing had muttered, with an apologetic smile. 'It's this world we live in that's to blame! But believe me, sir, I've come to make amends!'

Mr Lennard stared at him – and Mr Billing promptly declared his intention of turning King's Evidence! He knew where was the second murderer in brown and, for the usual consideration, was prepared to give him up. The 'usual consideration' was the sparing of his wretched life. Which, indeed, came to pass; for, though Mr Billing's heart was black as pitch, his plump lawyer's hands were still as clean as snow.

There was nothing the justice of the law could do with him but sentence him to three years in Newgate Gaol. Of which he served a month – and then fell an odd victim . . .

The old man who dwelt in the fireplace took a strong fancy to him and offered him Smith's old snoozing place. Which Mr Billing, being temporarily without friends, was very glad of, and slept there comfortably till, in one of the old man's dreadful twitchy nightmares, his head was stove in by the old man's chained wrists.

Naturally a great fuss was made, and it was strongly urged that the old man be sent to Bedlam as being a danger to himself and other prisoners. But he never went, for (and not for the first time) his son – to whom the State was much obliged – pleaded powerfully and successfully for his father to remain in the Stone Hall. His son was Mr Jones, the hangman . . . so the State could scarce refuse *him* . . .

For a while Smith and Mr Mansfield wondered uneasily if this strange and violent incident would affect Miss Mansfield – considering her one-time regard for the lying attorney. But Miss Mansfield was well out of that wood and, indeed, out of the wood that had shadowed most of her life.

Smith, staying as he did in Vine Street, had become so much Mr Mansfield's companion and friend that the tempestuous young lady found herself – as often as not – quite unnecessary. She was able to go out and about in the Town, where, by an extraordinary coincidence, she found a likeable young gentleman from Sussex who had been waiting for her all his life (though neither of them suspected it at first).

So Smith, despite his independence of pocket and spirit, has stayed on in Vine Street as firmly and cheerfully and contentedly as only a truly free spirit could have done. Nothing holds him but affection, and nothing feeds this affection so much as the deep understanding of his own fair situation in his blind friend's dark world.

Sometimes, of a late afternoon, the pair of them go out together, and stroll as far as Golden Square, where Smith tells Mr Mansfield how fine and prosperous a certain Establishment is looking these days. Then they go inside it, and Miss Bridget and Miss Fanny are pleased and charmed to serve them with chocolate. (Gin? The very idea! We are dealing now with ladies!) Then they go out again, and Smith looks up at the shop sign with a grin.

Miss Bridget and Miss Fanny. Court Dressmakers.

He nudges Mr Mansfield in the ribs.

'Oo's to know the Court they was makers for was the Criminal one at Old Bailey?'

And, from their fine bay window, the sisters smile and wave and watch their neat, small brother and his grand and gentle friend, walk side by side along the square, till at last they take the corner and are lost from sight.

But now the sun goes down and the air darkens. A wind sets in and clouds swing across the sky. Miss Fanny looks out somewhat sadly and dabs at her eyes with a piece of fine lace. She is thinking of Lord Tom and his glittering ways. But then she looks northward and sighs and smiles. For Lord Tom sleeps in a neat grave at the top of Highgate Hill, overlooking the Finchley Common. Nothing would have pleased him better . . . for from there 'tis but a ghost's step to visit Bob's Inn and go a-riding the night wind with Turpin, Robinson and Duval. A splendid and gallant company!